# Algier's Tomorrow

# Other Books by Blue Moon Authors

*Anonymous*
The Captive
My Secret Life

*Maria Madison*
The Reckoning
The Encounter
What Love

*Akahige Namban*
Woman of the Mountain, Warriors of the Town
Tokyo Story

*P.N. Dedeaux*
Clotilda
Transfer Point-Nice

*Richard Manton*
Departure from the Golden Cross
Elaine Cox
The Odalisque

*Edward Delaunay*
Beatrice
Between the Shadows and the Light

*Wilma Kauffen*
Our Scene
Virtue's Rewards

*Martin Pyx*
The Tutor's Bride
Summer Frolics

*Jack Spender*
Professor Spender and the Sadistic Impulse

*Don Winslow*
Ironwood
Ironwood Revisited

# Algier's Tomorrow

P. N. Dedeaux

BLUE MOON BOOKS, INC. NEW YORK

Copyright © 1993 by Blue Moon Books, Inc.

All Rights Reserved

No part of this book may be reproduced, stored in a retrievals system, or transmitted in any form, by any means, including mechanical, electronic, photocopying, recording or otherwise, without prior written permission of the publishers.

First Blue Moon Edition 1993

First Printing 1993

ISBN 1-56201-017-4

Manufactured in the United States of America

Published by Blue Moon Books, Inc.
PO Box 1040
Cooper Station, New York, NY 10276

*"If we avow that the senses' joy is always dependent upon the imagination, always regulated by the imagination, one must not be amazed by the numerous variations the imagination is apt to suggest during the pleasurable episode, by the infinite multitude of different tastes and passions the imagination's various extravagances will bring to light. However luxurious these tastes, they ought not to appear more remarkable than those of an ordinary species; there is no reason to find a meal-time eccentricity less extraordinary than a bedroom whim ... Three-quarters of the universe may find the rose's scent delicious without that serving either as evidence upon which to condemn the remaining quarter which might find the smell offensive, or as proof that this odor is truly agreeable."*

*de Sade*

# 1

"VIKKI. HE'S STARING AT YOU AGAIN."
"Who is?"
"Marshall."
"America's reason for Europe. Is *he* still waiting for Hemingway, too?"

The Hon. Victoria Digby stifled an inexistent yawn and slightly turned her perfect profile (all the way down) to gravely affix her enormous dark disks to the café's right, near the unspeakable john. Victoria was sixteen and a half, an English miss—her school enemies said in all senses—with short, licked-back black hair, a liquid little body coated now with tan to the insteps, and an upper figure that had more than once made her father, the irascible Earl, rush into his rose garden and prune down everything in sight to the dimensions of so many celery stalks. These curved, heavy, outward-thrusting mounds, so tense they might have been in milk, quite dried the old Earl's mouth of a sunny summer morning. Frankly, he swore they had stopped the sundial there. At any rate they were why he had allowed his only daughter abroad this year, to go where outsiders dwelt. So far as he was concerned, every male in the South of France was a rotter, but Vikki could look after herself all right. After all, was she not damn close to a black belt in judo? And, in any case, she was to be accompanied, chaperoned, by her good chum Joy, and had not Joy's rather imbecilic father, old ffrenchFox-Todde, been his fag at school as a boy?

At the moment Vikki's slick-skinned British beauties were unbrassiered under a white silk overblouse, for she had on a natty nautical number in the evening café. Her flippy little navy wool skirt was worn (perforce) over nothing, occasioning little squirms on the straight wicker chair, occasioning in turn a curious expressionless tension in the male public around her. The public around Victoria Digby was generally male, except at that unutterable school in Rutlandshire she still had to go to, under whose timbered roofs a quite incredible degree of feminine frustration worked itself up all term-time for discharge at intervals like this.

"Damnit, that's the third time that fake French Count

has dropped his matches right in front of our table, Joy. I can't help it if he sees my cunt. What does he expect? Feathers?"

"Marshall," came the answer from under the equally unseeing gaze beside her, the granny shades fixed also on the vista of shimmering sea and nodding yachts across the road, "likes to sit to one side of your bosom."

"The Bosom, please."

"And slightly behind my behind."

"The Behind, dear." The Bosom shot The Bottom an affectionate smile. "You have been a bloody idiot, haven't you, Joy?"

"I ser-s'pose so."

"And you are going to regret it, aren't you?"

"Yer-yes."

Joy ffrench (as she was popularly known at the fashionable school the girls frequented) dropped her white blonde head. Huge lashes covered her very violet eyes, which were constantly dewy and always looked just about to cry. Though only sixteen Joy was marvelously made in her way—which was bigger, heavier, more sumptuous, yet just as succulent as her present sister in sin; she had a flat, heart-shaped face with a little pointed chin that was about the only aspect of herself in common with her friend—unless you took into account the almost equally colossal chest. Her chief feature, however, was her positively Abyssinian rump, whose *ensellure,* today, was clad in the second epidermis of pale cuffless pants, lightly bell-bottomed, under an adorable dark sweater that hammocked the lazy sway of her luxuriously nippled and opulently unbrassiered bust. She looked frightened, and was so.

"All right," said Victoria with a sigh that overturned two pernods behind her, "let's go over it again. For the last time. You lost your purse and you lost our panties."

"I can't help it if he took our . . . underthings, Vic," was the pouted reply. "I don't understand it, really."

"Looks a lot like one of those lost morsels he's using now, to blow his moron nose with." Victoria conceded but the briefest flicker of her lids in the direction of the crew-cut and actor's stock expression of the slim young American sitting watching them. "Did he try to make you again last night, Joy dearie?"

"I don't care to be back-scuttled, thanks," said the bigger girl, sniffily.

"No one's perfect, love."

The Café Beau Soleil at Ste. Maxime was filling up. It was the apéritif hour and the pilgrims were coming off the beaches at the chainless ends of their cigarettes like so many weary penitents. White Russians, black Americans, a brown Dane (flicker of recognition in quickly locked eyes—God, what a prick!) accompanying his latest philosophic concubine—Victoria Digby watched them stroll out of the damaging sun and make the dreadful search for their usual tables, and snappy pernods, and it was quite unbearable to think that they would all go on being here while she and Joy would not. They had come to the end of their cash, which, in Ste. Maxime at any rate, was the same thing as time. Their little screw-happy paradise in the sun had suddenly run out. It was all too cruel. She could already count three stiff cocks that had been up her here. And right up her, too. She grew medium-to-moist at the very thought.

And it was all Joy's silly fault. They had stepped out two days ago to a cosmetic store to buy some mad mascara and the idiot had forgotten to lock the door of their room. Someone must have been following them, right enough, since when they returned two minutes and one Coke later Joy's handbag had been stolen—her own had thankfully been over her lean, tanned left wrist—as also, not entirely unrelatedly although surprisingly, the little line of panties they had strung across the bathroom after a bidet laundering. What was worse, all their passports and tickets had been leaking out of Joy's bag like so many hungry tongues. What was worse than that, they were already due back home. And school.

All they had left was their flippant clothes, a pair of pantyhose each (currently drying from the shower-rail), and a most ardent desire not to leave all this blissful sunlight . . . and general bliss, for bucketsful of British rain. Victoria rapped her mental knuckles.

"Christ on fucking crutches, is there absolutely no way? No, there isn't, is there. It's the nine-forty from Orly and ghastly Aunt Grizel at the godawful airport, to guarantee us. Oh hell, you need a spanking, Joy, and you know it."

"Since we're overdue as is, I all too strongly fear I shall get one. From Mummy, when I'm back."

"And I'll bet the idea makes your little pit all itchy-bitchy right now, doesn't it. I get mine from Daddy. The lecher."

She sighed again, and a Peruvian ex-Cossack dancer nearby gulped like a porpoise. The male eyes roved over them like so many parents, in fact, reclaiming their young.

"Not to mention school," said Joy.

"Play up School," said Victoria, with sudden solemnity.

"Play up School," echoed her comrade in adversity, rather more hollowly. "I say, you couldn't go just one more *café et cognac*, eh Vic?"

Victoria rummaged in her purse. A waiter appeared

too quickly. He leant over her shoulder. The well-bred girl tried to do up a button of her blouse, by no means an easy task.

"Two coffees."

"And two cognacs," added Joy sweetly.

"And perhaps one brioche . . . *avec*."

"*Mais* certainly, Madame," said the Irish help instantly.

"Are you sure today's Saturday, Vic? That it's really tomorrow we have to go?"

"Sweetie, I quite forgot to check with my sec."

She was occupied by the fact that some unseen appreciator of beauty behind was making this big deal about exiting through the crowded tables, his knee lingering long over the cheeky curves of the British mini bouncing back from Victoria's chair.

"There," she said a trifle nostalgically, watching this hero leaving with one hand on the tightly beshorted ass of his latest lush Latin, "goes dear Giorgio with his straight white teeth, and straight hard prick, and he'll never rape us again."

"It's really too tough. And, as you say, *hard*."

"And to think. With your bottom . . . ."

"And your bosom."

"God, what it was like to be young."

The waiter had returned and Victoria's cute black crop swung over the smallest glass on the Riviera around which he had just slopped bad brandy.

"Do I sense Marshall coming over? I like to be rimmed, but I've never been buggered and I don't think I care to be, thanks."

"Me too. Ugh." She added softly, "It makes me want to go."

"So you have been, Joy?"

But further converse on the topic was cut off by the arrival of the lean, bronzed and very tightly jean-clad youth, who could water ski as well as he could fight bulls in Spain. Marshall Dexter grinned and let his trembling fingers rest lightly on Victoria's well-padded shoulder.

"How's the jut set?" he quipped, looking down at the rubbery nubs pressing through the shirt and sweater. "Fit to bust?"

"Marshall, might you take your bones off my . . . shoulder. Thanks."

"You wouldn't pay for our drinks, would you?" suggested equally unencouraging Joy.

"Sorry, darlings, as usual I haven't a cent."

"As usual."

"God."

"I'm hungry," pouted Joy, looking at some enviably well-fed, sandalled conquest coming off the beach in her bikini. "I haven't eaten all day."

"That's what I call an atomic bikini," said the lad, his eyes following the figure in the last lancing sun. "Fifty percent fall-out."

"Very funny, I'm sure."

"I guess she could laugh it all off, at that."

They watched a tense Argentinian millionaire leave his table and follow the girl in an epicene trot.

"Disgusting," said the girls.

"Disgustingly rich," murmured Marshall, insinuating himself between The Bottom and The Bosom, and duly admiring both. "That one can buy you . . . oh, about a third of the gold in the world. And that," he concluded with a rotten-fruit flourish, "makes all the difference between a bell and a belle."

"What's that?" said Joy mechanically.

"Well, you see, a bell rings with a ding, but a belle has to have a dong. Especially in the South of France." He added, "That's to say in the south."

Victoria had waxed pensive at the wisecrack.

"He looks exactly like an ungrateful turtle to me," she said. Then she drained her dregs and added, "It is possible Joy might like to meet him."

"I was convinced she would."

"Who? What?" Joy sat up straight, sending all sorts of things swinging. "Me?" she gulped like Chicken Little.

"Is she really forty?" said Victoria ruminatively.

"She doesn't even look twenty," snapped Joy, in confusion, staring from one to the other of them. "What are you two talking about here?"

"Forty DD," admitted Marshall gently, staring at the colossal aureoles of the older girl's chest, whose crenellations were quite clearly visible under her silk. "Josito likes big things . . . like, like, well oil wells, and steel mills, and sugar plantations . . . ."

"And bananas," said Victoria.

"Of course."

"Natch."

"Put an s on that, and you're in, my dear."

But the girl had an idea and it was causing her to frown. She dribbled out some tinny francs on the table.

"Do you really have to go?" asked Marshall, edging ever closer. Hell, he could see . . . he could almost swear he could see, down in the valley between those hillocks borne so beautifully free, one small wisp of hair. It excited him intensely. If he pulled it, would she clutch her twat? Or what? "I mean there's this absurd rumor of you two adorables having to leave tomorrow? For England, I mean. Are you sure we couldn't talk this over?" He gestured ambitiously at the garçon, but no one came. "I mean, like if it's bread you need you could always model for me."

"Ha ha."

"Do you think," said Joy coyly, "we might recite poetry, and pass the hat? They do in San Francisco."

"If you did it in the altogether," the boy began, but Victoria had stood suddenly, almost defiantly, up and a respectful hush descended on the denizens of the Café Beau Soleil, which caught the evening sun at Ste. Maxime.

"Joy, we have to toddle," she said.

As she undulated out in her micro to the cobbles, many grievous male eyes fastened on the rhythmically bounding elasticities under the swinging pleats. The younger girl followed her, bumping into one or two tin tables as she went, but they were softish bumps.

"If you need me," the youth called after them, "I'll be around."

"Not my arse you won't," muttered Victoria to herself. But she had had an idea, and apart from that there were things to do. Exciting things. To Joy. "Come along, dear," she said, taking her junior's senior wrist, "let's get this over with."

"What over with?" asked the other suspiciously.

And the only answer maliciously returned to that was—"As if you didn't know."

## 2

AS JOY FOLLOWED HER FRIEND UP THE NARROW stairs to their rented room, the latter's sailor skirt flipped from side to side and the former had a vision of a marvelously fatted ass, doing just the same. The sulcal fold snapped under each chubby cheek as Victoria mounted and Joy apprehensively ran a hand over her own prominent posterior, moving under its thin cloth. She was afraid that she knew only too well.

The vision of the girl ahead was of a scene behind, in all senses. Bothington College was probably the most desirable and expensive (and desirable because expensive) ladies' academy in England, or the world, for that matter. So select it seemed to have a waiting list for centuries, it consisted of a grim Gothic mansion in a very cold corner of the universe, a small English county where it rained almost continually and upper-class girls were brought up to be brides of the House of Lords, and perhaps of the Foreign Office. It was indeed so hideously snobbish that it could afford to be a sort of uncertified prison—an asylum in all senses, as more than one long-suffering girl had put it, the motto and maxim of which was quite definitely spare-the-rod. If these sixty-odd debutantes-to-be were going to have a privileged and easy life in later years, well then, ran the common consensus of their parents, they should *go through it* now. Bothington was a living anachronism in swinging England, and amongst other things believed belligerently in corporal chastisement.

It was when she had been made a Prefect two terms before that Victoria had become fully conscious of the younger girl's presence. Under the school uniform, paradoxically longer-skirted than those minis the girls bought and wore in Carnaby Street in the holidays, Joy's sensuous bottoms rolled alliciantly; the tight navy stuff hugged her hips under the broad leather belt, making the girl resemble a bottle of chartreuse from behind—well filled. Victoria had become somehow more and more conscious of Joy's beauty, and beautiful rump. If she'd been born a man, she frankly admitted, she'd have been an assman. Joy's round calves, perpetually tanned, it seemed, led up to slim knees and heavy, wobbly hips so sturdily full of youth she longed at times to grab them in her hands—and pull. With a little quiver of excitement Victoria knew she had to see them under punishment.

Prefects at Bothington were not allowed personally to beat, but they could, as monitors of various activities, report small offenses and thus get a girl ordered c.p. (or corporal punishment)—or a *swiping,* as it was called. Consequently it was not long before Joy found herself inscribed on the bleak little list that was put up on the noticeboard outside Great Hall, and was eyed with alarm by two or three sinners a night:

*The following will attend on the Duty Mistress in the Gymnasium after Evening Prep tonight;*
Archer, Jane
Carvel, the Lady Barbara
ffrench-Fox-Todde, Joy.

Promptly at nine, when prep broke up and the most junior girls (or minnies) went to bed, the others having a free half-hour or more, the three culprits put their books away and repaired to a windy wing of the mansion, where they waited in a line outside the gymnasium door, having first changed into P.T. (or Physical Training) rig—a brief mint-green tunic caught in at the waist with a golden girdle, or elastic school belt. Three trim, tense, but alas rather trembling tookies over six knocking knees.

"Is Sandy really Duty tonight?"

"Cripes, she canes so tight."

"And low."

"If anyone can get in the fold, *she* can."

"You can say that again, Barby."

"I want to wee-wee."

"Well, you can't, so there."

"About all you can do, my dear Jane, is grin and b-a-r-e it."

"Well, I'm jolly well going to try not to let her see how much it stings."

"Bravo you, Joy."

"Play up School."

"Play up School," the other two automatically, if a little hollowly, re-echoed.

"Here they come."

For the two Pre's responsible for their several appearances were now swinging down the passage, arm in arm, humming the school song—Helen Elstir and our inexorable Victoria, her tie quite lost between the girth of her great thrusting and aggressive breasts. These came to rest in front of the unlooking, so wretched, rank.

"Feeling nice and shivery behind, Janey?" Helen Elstir's well-manicured hand slipped under the tail of one tunic and felt there for a second. She it was who had reported the first two girls for Lates—both having been infinitesimally late for chapel service. "I do hear as there are some new canes, and Sandy's been on tip-top form all this half. I fear me ten is going to hurt like hell."

The girl addressed, a mousy-haired, rather plain seventeen-year-old of chunky build, said nothing, staring ahead. She alone was repeating, the other two being eighters. Each Bothington Beauty got eight strokes her first offense in a term, ten the second, and twelve the third. More than this had not for a long time been heard of, twelve in the gym being such a test that it seemed to bring the most stubborn to her senses, extra cuts being added for flinching, wincing or getting up before Permission, the ritual word to rise.

Victoria contemplated the clefted rump filling the matching panties of her particular victim, as she lifted the little tunic skirt behind.

"Well, there's plenty of room for stick here. Are you well walloped at home, scum?"

"Yes, Digby."

"Bend down and touch your toes and let me feel this mighty pair. Mmmm. I shall advise a really wide spread. The cane is an impact instrument and to do justice to these chubbies . . . ."

"It will have to make *impact*," gurgled Helen Elstir happily, seizing her colleague's arm and drawing her to the gymnasium door. This the pair entered grinning like twin Cheshire cats, for theirs was the task of preparing the scene of action. "Exciting, isn't it."

"I just wanted to make sure she hadn't soaped," unnecessarily explained Victoria, "or been sitting on stone, or one of those tricks the scum get up to."

"Lovely lovely scummy butts. Do you think Sandy will cut them *quite* in two?"

"All I know is, it will hurt them more than it will her."

Giggling and chuckling, they got the big room ready. The great gaunt gym was enlivened by a flickering fire one end, and it was in front of this the girls dragged out the horse used for beating—low, but not too. Next, they took two canes from a closet and put them on a deal table to one side. These instruments—bendy, but not too—were a long round yellow, thrillingly living in their whip and flick, perfectly made for punishment from their well-waxed knob-like grip to the tip which, in the best of British pedagogical tradition, was slightly thickened for . . . impact.

Helen was making juicy swishes through the air with one of these, and breathing deeply, when the door opened to admit the smiling, striding Duty Mistress, black book in one hand.

"Good evening, Miss Nicholson," they both respectfully chimed, dropping a knee in the best Bothington curtsey.

"Let's see, let's see, who have we here?"

The Duty Mistress invariably put on tennis attire for this exacting job, freedom of movement being essential in caning upper-class behinds, and Sandra (Sandy) Nicholson looked the part to the T, which was how she stood now, in her squelchy sneaks, her arms thrust sideways in a catlike stretch or warming-up exercise. She was thirty-five with a close-cut carroty crop of hair, an impish grin for her years, and very strong wrists and thighs—she had been a high-diving champ in her day, some sort of Scottish junior wizard. She enjoyed caning and made no bones about it; having come from the extremely lower depths of Glasgow, what's more, nothing gave her more pleasure than to make an Earl's daughter, say, twist and writhe for her life under a scalding, carefully drawn-out eighter, and then add, after the girl had shown heroic stoicism, the ritual three extra (master's cuts, as they were sometimes called) for flinching. Her bright eyes now ran over the list in the book she had opened on the table; it was big as a Bible and twice as frightening, containing a veritable Burke's Peerage of beaten bottoms within its covers.

"Hm, hm, all eighters, I take it."

"Alas, I grieve to say," said Helen Elstir with a hypocritic tut-tut motion of her blunt-cut brown locks, "Jane Archer is a second comer."

"I see, I see. Well then," said the grinning matron, glancing up, "let's see if we can't send her out with a rather more *punctual* pair of buttocks, shall we just." She seized a cane and in a motion that made both watching girls swallow flexed it double on one thigh. "Place 'em for me nice and tight, and I want the tunics well up their backs. Nothing more distracting than clothing coming down. Take your time about it, though, it does their souls good to wait it out a bit."

"Yes, Miss Nicholson."

"This Joy ffrench-Todde," said Victoria with demurely lowered gaze, "I do respectfully suggest the most extreme severity in her case. She's been snotty and uppity all term long."

"Too big for her britches, eh?" The mistress' eyes gave a gimlet gleam.

"Exactly, Miss. Needs bringing down a peg."

"I'll bring her down eight. I'll take the eighters first, and then Jane. Bring in that Barbara, would you, Helen."

The Prefect strode to the door which she opened, calling, "Carvel."

The Lady Barbara Carvel, very tall, lean black-haired and ashen-faced, a sterling seventeen-year-old most of whom was leg, jiggle-joggled across to the area of operations.

"You are about to be beaten for being late. Have you anything to say?"

"No," replied the girl rather distantly.

"Then I am afraid I shall have to give you eight." The mistress thrashed the air with a sickening sound and shivered the young flesh standing expressionlessly to attention before her. "Of the best. You know, really, Barbara, if you walk around with your nose in the air like that, you risk sticking it into someone's eye. Well. What are you waiting for? I have an idea you aren't going to be needing your pants for the next few minutes, my dear."

Rather hectically the tall girl bent and slipped two thumbs in the elastic under her tunic. She took off her panties, folded them neatly and put them on a stool.

"You didn't wet them, did you?"

"No, Miss."

Helen Elstir examined the miniscule apology of a garment. "No, Miss Nicholson, she didn't soil her panties."

"Good. I was wondering if her expression was due to some nasty smell about. But I think it will change after eight stripes across her backside, don't you."

"Most certainly, Miss Nicholson."

"Put her over, please."

Helen Elstir drew the girl to the horse and bent her over it. Since its leather-padded upper level had been lowered at the head for this important work, Lady Carvel was arse up, her legs parted, and her head sunk between her outstretched arms. Slowly she was bared, her belt being loosened and her tunic pushed up her ribs almost to her armpits. Watching, Victoria felt a very definite butterfly of excitement flutter in her stormpit.

The girl's legs were lean and raced, beautifully beveled, with thighs so sinuous they merged imperceptibly into the neat, high hips above. Between these a very full, hairy lump of flesh thrust back, its furrow hidden in its forest. The mistress stared at the spectacle a second.

"Well, I suppose one shouldn't expect a billiard ball," she got out at last. "All the same, I think I'll have those legs a little closer, if you will, Helen. Thanks."

She wanted to make sure the cane made cruel contact with the full width of underbum, behaired as this was beneath. She stepped back, frowned, pranced a pace and thoughtfully lashed the licky rod across the muscleless meat. The girl gasped.

"One," said Helen Elstir. Victoria rubbed her leg. A wide weal had sprung up, dark red on the left and inky on the right.

*Thlckk!*

The mistress sliced again. A convulsive ripple ran along the thighs as Helen drawled out, "Two. Brace back your knees."

Victoria looked up at the second hand of the great clock above the fireplace. Sandy was really excellent. She hit so hard she could afford up to a quarter-minute intervals. With luck this would go on two whole minutes.

*Thrrrwhlckkk!*

"Three."

They seemed to have covered the narrow, clenching ass. And five more still to come.

"Relax them," said Helen, from the girl's head. "Push it up or you'll get extra."

"Jesus!" the girl said, after the next. Her head came back and she gave a short, sharp fart. Then she lay shuddering on the horse, awaiting the next. It was a long time coming and when it did seemed to whip right through her. The last three hit into beaten flesh low down and the girl took them half-erect. She called out "Christ!" each time.

"Get right down," said Helen with dislike.

Her can contorted like a burly-queen's for a while, until the mistress smilingly said, "Permission."

The girl leapt up, clutching her well-streaked chubbies, and writhed her way to recover her panties.

"Feeling a little warmer now, behind, Barbara? I'm afraid you'll have to write for me five hundred times, 'I must not swear under punishment.'"

"Yes, Miss Nicholson."

"Stinging?"

"Ghastly." Fluttering fingers drew up apologetic panties. "Th-that's the tightest I've had here."

"Well it'll get worse for half a minute, then remain about the same for some three, so I shouldn't delay your exit. Send Joy, will you."

Victoria had been watching in a trance, entranced. Collecting herself, she realized she had to go into action: this was her charge.

"Untidy locker . . . report of Prefect Digby . . . have you anything to say?"

"No, Miss."

"Bend this Amazon over, please."

She did so, parting the legs in a wide spread. Even then, so lushly fatted was Joy's pride, the curve of cheeks continued to the thighs and only a sleekly slotted vulval fig, like a miniature football in shape, quivered back at them. As Miss Nicholson drew a respectful distance back, Victoria's misbehaving hands shot between her legs; she knew she was longing, absolutely aching with delight, to see that fleshy basin cut into . . . again and again. It was simply made for the cane.

And well caned it was. Joy took her tanning like a trooper, albeit she squirmed her front pitifully against its leathern rest, and ooohed and aaahed in most mellifluous octaves. She danced when it was done, and tripped and sat, and they laughed. But Victoria had her beady eye on the sill of the horse, whose leather looked most definitely dampened, where Joy had been.

But if Joy had been well caned, brave chunky Jane Archer was cut to pulp. For some reason the mistress attacked these stocky mounds with hostility, hitting viciously. Three, four, five . . . the girl had asked to take off her glasses and looked back sightlessly in her pain . . . pluckily she stuck to it, got to eight, begged for a rest, took the ninth holding the horse as if it were a lifeboat, swallowed, somehow, the tenth and jumped up, clutching and hopping.

"Getting up before Permission."

She looked round wildly as the two Prefects advanced upon her. This time they held her over, one hand on one shoulder, while the cringing bottom absorbed three slicy "master's strokes." A butcher's dozen, and the wicked culprit left the big room moaning, almost feeling her poor way forward.

"Next time it's twelve, and 'twon't be so easy."

Sweating, the mistress slapped her sides, signed and closed her book, and followed after. Helen and Victoria were left to tidy up.

"God, that was terrif. Wasn't it, Vikki?"

"Unbelievable."

"Weren't those last three beauts? But the way she waled into Barbara. I think that was my favorite. I love a nervy ass, it seems to hurt them so much more. Which was your preference, darling?"

"Joy," said Victoria, barely daring to breathe.

"You know, someone seems to have come on the horse. Look, it's all gummy."

"And scummy."

"Would it be my imagination, or was that . . . ."

"That was Joy," said Victoria, shortly. She held her own legs tight together. Helen sidled to her.

"Oh God, Vikki, I've always so admired you. These fantastic breasts you have. I don't know how you keep them up so."

"United we stand, divided we fall," quipped Victoria, almost snorting. She was going to come any minute if she wasn't careful.

"Are they really forty-one?"

"Over the nipple, or over the aureole?"

Helen Elstir slung one arm around them. "Angel, there's something I've always wanted. Please."

"What?"

"Do me a favor. Let me give you a couple."

"No," said Victoria decidedly.

"Please. Just two. I know who has a vibrator. For after. What do you think Sandy's doing to herself right now?"

But Victoria had refused and kept instinctively out of other's way for the rest of that term. Then in the last week it had happened.

She had been unable to detect the derriere of her desire in any very mortal sin, until the night she had had stayed up on purpose, tiptoed along the upper landing and caught Joy and another girl talking after lights out in their dormitory.

"Follow me," she said, beckoning bleakly, in the light of her torch.

The twin sinners had stood disconsolately enough, in their pyjamas and dressing gowns, as Victoria addressed them in her personal, prefectorial study, or den. She had on a skimpy sweater and soft tartan pants, extremely close-fitting. Elasticized until they were snug as gloves, Victoria's slacks were always very special.

"You know perfectly well, you two," she hectored uncertainly, avoiding their eyes and pacing prominently before them, "that by rights I should report this to tomorrow's Duty Mistress and you'd both get a royal licking. By the by, you weren't masturbating, were you, either of you? Judy? Joy?"

"No, Digby."

"No."

"Very well. I'm offering you an alternative. You can take it from me now—ten apiece, or you can wait to get it tomorrow night from Miss Sweeney. Which?"

Her nipples butted at the fabric as she faced them. She was flushing hard, since she knew it was extremely risky for a Prefect to take the law into her own hands like this. Consequently her corpuscles were giving a steady dance up her pulses. "Which?" she again thundered in her best no-nonsense tone of voice.

"I'll take it from you, thanks, Digby," said Judy Sharrington, a thin, dark-haired girl with a sloping bottom.

"I'll get it over with too," Joy had agreed in a hollow echo; and Victoria had been out of the room in a flash, her flash in fact lighting her to the empty gym where she filched a cane. The great grey manor was sleeping, it was plain, and no one would trouble them in the wing where the Prefects' studies were.

When she returned both girls were standing in the same place, both looking a little more disconsolate, and Joy twiddling her dressing gown cord in her fingers.

"You wait outside," she was told by the frowning senior, "and you—take off your gown, drop your britches and bend over here."

The willowy cane pointed, pressing with eager elasticity at a spot in the flooring to one side; the girl shuffled forward, feet fettered in wrinkled Viyella, and touched her toes like a hinge. She had nice snub buttocks with quite a bit of give and Victoria was beginning to feel thoroughly alive. The illicit nature of the activity was like a tonic to her senses and her nerves flared fire as she saw the upside-down eyes of the little brunette clench tight in anticipation. She drew back and aimed like a golfer on the tee.

Whhhh-rrrrpp!

The parted curtain of air made by the cane was more menacing than the dry snap of impact. The girl gasped, but no more. A sullen weal flamed up. Victoria continued slowly, but for a time only the whippy travel of the rod up her striking arm responded to her half-fearful excitement, visible in her plangently pulsing nips and widely opened nostrils.

Victoria hit harder. Suddenly at the seventh, the girl panted and rubbed her shins with pain. It was highly satisfactory. But despite all she could do the stalwart Prefect could extract no further honey from her victim. After the tenth had whunked in she said "All right" in a bored voice, and turned off.

It was when she turned back again she got her reward. The girl was arched erect, her face squeezed up, and clasping under her well-hit hams as if a horde of hornets had just been unloosed there. Victoria goggled. The sight dried her throat with sudden sensation. She knew that this was very pleasing, indeed.

"I'm s-s-sorry," said the wounded one gaspingly, still wrestling and doubting, "but it was . . . you did . . . ker-cane me so terrifically tight, Digby."

"Good. Let that be a lesson to you, scum. Adjust your dress, don't say anything about this to anyone, and get out. Send in Joy."

She was glad to note that the culprit went out still gasping and holding her posterior portions as if for dear life, behind. Joy, entering, was not unobservant of this exit; she was looking very white indeed, and her violet eyes seemed enormous.

"Take them down. Ten."

It was when Victoria saw her prey standing there a moment later, with hung head and twisting hands in front, wearing no more than a short pyjama jacket of pale stuff, that she knew what true sexual excitement was. Joy was the perfected victim, or shepherdess—all penitent poke, dimity, expectant of the briny birch or stick. Standing behind her Victoria took a very deep breath; she knew she was in the presence of greatness.

"Bend over with your hands on your knees."

"With m-my hands on my . . . ?"

"Don't repeat what I say. Do it. I'm going to cane you hard."

She did. She cut up into the complacent curves of the slabby underbuttocks. Like this she could watch them joggle as she hit. She drew it out slowly, seeing Joy look wretchedly round for each next—Thwuwuwuwuck!

"Play up School," she said once, encouragingly.

At the eighth pelting cut Joy stood up, whining with pain, squirming in her hands a second.

"I'm sorry," she too obediently said, "but that her-hit . . . the same spot."

When it was all over Victoria watched her jump and dance, her spasmic trounces almost lewd as she bucked to beat the pain. She herself was beginning to feel faint behind the eyes and stood facing the wall a second, heart heaving. She was dimly aware that Joy was dressing. But not leaving. Why not?

There came a small sound—"Are you sure you don't want to give me extra, Digby? I mean, for getting up."

"No, no," Victoria said hoarsely. "Out."

She leant against the wall. She too was begging breath, and barely saw the door open and the girl in the skimpy mini slink sarcastically in and close it behind her.

"Well, well, well, three holes in the ground," the newcomer said mockingly. "Or somewhere or other. I wonder what the Head would say, Vikki old bean, if she knew you'd just caned two minors without permission. Care to bet?"

It was Helen Elstir. Victoria looked at her in horror. This time her blood really roared in her mind.

"What are you doing here, Helen? You wouldn't be sneaking, would you?"

"It really was repulsively undignified when Marcia Moore got that public birching last half, wasn't it, Vic dear? Couldn't even contain her water, in front of the whole school. My oh my. Those on the right side said that her . . . right side . . . looked like a lump of uncooked beef before it was over. Really, too much. An unesthetic. But that was only three dozen. A Bothington Pre exceeding her rights in this manner would be bound to get four, as well as stripped of all privileges."

"Witch," said Victoria, understanding and blanching in her turn now, "I could throw you around this room like so much kindling, Helen, and send out your guts as spaghetti. And you know it. When do I start? Now?"

She did her best to glare, but Helen Elstir was quite composed. She had even accepted the cane from Victoria's unfeeling fingers.

"Beat me up as much as you like, dearie. I'd still tell the Head tomorrow, and get Judy and Joy to come with me too. Pity. Be so nice to have the term over and the whole matter forgotten, wouldn't it."

Finally Victoria said, "What do you want, then? What's your bargain, you bitch?"

"Simple. I want your bottom bent over the end of that table, dear heart, while I wale into it with ten of the very tightest. Only fair. It's what you did give each of them." She flicked her calf with the stick and ouched dramatically. "Christ, I've been dreaming of caning the can off you, Vic, and it's either that or probable expulsion. After a public birching."

Victoria said. "I keep on my slacks. I don't have anything on beneath."

"Then you get twelve," came the sweetly smiling answer, "to compensate."

"Beast." Victoria's fingers fumbled with one side of her trews. These were soon in quite miserable wrinkles at her ankles. "All right, let's get on with it, then." Having fisted that cane herself, she was feeling extremely frightened now.

But Helen was standing with head to one side, and this quite maddening smile stuck on her farded face.

"Frig yourself first. Come on. I mean it. Just in case. I'm not having you enjoy this, Victoria."

"Helen, please."

"Come on. Frig your clit. I want to see it all ooozy and juicy before we start. And I'm checking your pulse rate to see that you really come, too." She took Victoria's disengaged wrist and put a finger on its quivery veins inside. "Start tossing yourself off, baby."

There was silence in the room then but for a vague sloshy sound. Victoria said in her most dignified tone, "I can't . . . I don't know . . . I can't get it now . . . ."

"Here. Let me try."

And almost at once she was on tiptoe, cursing and hissing, as the climax struck her and she jammed her thighs on Helen's worrying finger.

"Hey. I didn't say drown me, darling. By George, you go a lot. Now then, wasn't that nice? Just as well, 'cos this is going to be nasty. Bend over that table, with your bottom toward me, if you would."

Victoria lay limply at right angles, her legs together and braced back. She was damned if she would let Helen see her suffering. She hid her face between her arms, still panting fiercely. She felt the cold touch of wood on her skin.

"This is delightful. Arch it up a little more, would you, ducky. I say, your slot is sopping."

Thhhwlick!

"Hhhhhh . . . !"

*Thwlikkkkkkkkkkk!*

Two hoooh au she Christ can't God how it n-o-o-o-h *three* and seven to au au *foh-ur* a-u-i-eee how does she expect me to God God she's . . . fiiyyyve!

"Darling, you really are hairy, aren't you."

"Get on with it."

"Anything to oblige."

SihihiX! Au je it can't get a-a-a-h any worse and OOOOOH Seven . . . noooooh . . . *eight*. . . !

"Are you going to Queen Charlotte's Ball at the Dorchester next week, Vic?"

"If you must know, yes!"

"I'll be there. Wouldn't it be fun to introduce you to my brother and say, 'You've no idea how comic Victoria looks with dark red stripes across her ass, all jiggling and jumping.'"

"Helen, *please*. Cane me."

"So you want it now, huh."

THWRLUPPP!

"OW!" Victoria half rose after the fiendish cut which seemed to drive right through her seat: she staggered, whirling from the table and clutching her offended anatomy. "God alive, that was unf-f-f-f—"

She couldn't complete the word for pain. As a matter of fact she was scared she was going to cry. And there stood Helen, grinning like an idiot, feet astride with the cane bent back across her thighs, watching it and loving it.

"It's three extra for getting up before Permission."

Victoria glared at her furiously. "I can't take any more, Helen. You can't make me." She added in another tone, "Please."

Helen Elstir thought. She was enjoying this very much. She cocked her head to one side.

"Okay, I'll make a deal. Three more, or the Scum Kiss. Take your pick. Or, of course, the Head first thing tomorrow morning."

Victoria groaned. She was holding the hot coals of her cheeks with considerable respect for the other's aim.

"Please no more with the cane, Helen."

"Then?"

"I'll take the latter," said Victoria, with avoided eyes. The sooner this was over the better.

"You remember the Scum Kiss, of course."

"The latter," said Victoria stubbornly.

"Goody." And the girl jumped round at once, dropping the cane, pushing out her bottom, naked under the ridiculous mini which she pulled up. Then she grasped her twin cubs and hauled them apart. Victoria saw the puckered silk of the anus stretched till the rubbery ring of sphincter stood out with a sliver of entrail on display within.

"You place the beginning of the gut to the end of the gut, don't you," Helen Elstir was saying, easing herself forward a little on her parted flamingo limbs. "Play up, School. And if you have any butter in here, dip your tongue in it first, would you, Vic. I want it right up and kept there, or else. Kneel on your hands, please."

"This is utterly disgusting, Helen, and you know it," the big girl said, making for a closet with one hand still ruminating over her punished right side. She had kicked off her slacks and was bush-bare in front, a sturdy T of growth whose upper bar, curly, cropped and dry, crossed close under her navel. Having wet her tongue on the best dairy butter in Rutlandshire, she knelt behind the straddling tormentress. For a second she paused, then her pause turned into a frown of concentration and her face went forward on its task.

Helen gasped at once. The toe of one finger began to butt at her button. "Come on. Deeper in than that."

"Mmnnngh."

"No, I'm sure you can get it higher than that, Vic. Hell, my fag can. Stick it up . . . up . . . yerrs, *that's* better now. That's bliss." She gave a hippy wiggle, Victoria stuck to her task, and soon there were categoric stirrings above. The lovely young puppy flesh that was the glib junction of hip and thigh pressed across her chin and neck. "Christ . . . yes . . . God I could cane you all night long, you know it, angel . . . oh oh oh . . . now keep it UP!" Suddenly she tscked and said, "Right up I mean, Victoria. Now. You know what a brown nose is."

Doing her best to retain some last vestiges of maidenly dignity, Victoria objected—"Helen, please. You can't ask me to do that. I did it once when I was scum and I was sneezing shit for a week. Please."

"It's that, or else." Victoria's eyes were led by the other's to the exclamation point of the cane, from which they returned to the avid amber bud above. "In fact, I think I'm probably going to give you three more for size anyway."

Victoria took a deep breath and closed her eyes. The sooner this was over the better.

"Totally repulsive," she said, leaning forward.

Helen obligingly held apart her hams and suddenly, sooner than she'd expected, Victoria felt her feline nostrils nipped. Helen instantly sighed from her depths and a sudden scalding spasm there fortunately soon sent Victoria, kneeling on her hands, reeling. Helen shook like a dervish in her rut.

"Oh oh oh oh Goooooooooood, what *utter* heaven!"

Great gobs of her goo fell steaming to the ground.

"Play up School," said Victoria, modestly regaining her trousers. "I think I'll just take this cane back now if you don't mind." And she had left the room quickly, without further trouble.

# 3

"ENJOYING THE VIEW?" VICTORIA SWIRLED from the top of the stair. "Getting flip with my skirt?"

"It . . . *is* rather short, Vikki, you must admit." Joy blushed, her head bowing. In the skinny, sleazy little black sweater her breasts gave an apprehensive, or mildly yearning, judder.

"Everything in shape down there?"

"You've got an absolutely glorious b.t.m., and you know it, Vic."

"Not bad for The Bosom, if not as big as The Bottom. When I swiped you at school I wondered if you'd been buggered. That chinkhole's so inviting. But so, too, is your twat."

"Oooh, wouldn't it be gorgeous to have something sliding up it now!"

"Come along, said the spider to the fly." Victoria held open the door at the end of the landing, and tapped the passing butt as it came slinking by. It made a nice taut tap, all in all. Rayon gabardine, perhaps, and fairly bursting at its seams.

"After all, it was you who lost our panties."

It was a nice cheerful chintzy room in a quiet backstreet, off the old port, and Victoria locked the door as they went in, tossing her purse on a couch. She drew the sunny curtains, opened a closet door and appeared to be searching, somewhat on the floor.

"What are you doing, Vic?" the bigger girl asked dubiously.

The answer came back in the tone of the Head Prefect its owner was almost certainly destined to be—"I told you you needed a spanking and now I'm going to give you one."

"Oh, please, you don't have to."

"Oh, yes I do. Hell, if I'd only brought a riding switch. Guess this'll have to do. To start with."

"To start with!"

For Victoria was advancing purposefully with a thongy sandal in one hand, her right, holding it securely by the supple folded sole. The heel, however, as Joy knew since it was her own, was far from soft. It was hard. Very. It would hurt.

"Please, Vikki, please. You don't have to spank me. It wasn't my fault."

"Come on. You know you love it."

"I hate it. It's so . . . stingy, and awful."

"And you come rivers afterwards, don't you."

"Please." The girl gave a last, lost, pretty backward look at the menace behind her, her eyes seeming as ever ready to cry, then she asked, "How many?"

The sole rapped so hard on the outside of Victoria's own thigh she made herself wince.

"Twenty."

"Twenty!"

"Each side."

"Pur-lease!"

"Only, as the walls of this dump are like glass and

we don't want half of France's Finest rushing to your rescue, I'll give you them over your slacks. Pull them up tight and bend over the end of the bed. Quick.''

Joy did as bid, albeit somewhat slowly and reluctantly. With her hands resting on the low, modern double-bed her tender buns looked their imperial best. The thin, light-colored stuff of the bell-bottoms clung to their sturdy contours without so much as a crease from the knees on up. And it was this area that interested her roommate, pausing in admiration now. On Joy the fat was padded high and firm, it was altogether a meaty pair that awaited the punishment, the pulp of fruit visible at the bottom of the quivery division.

"Gad, you do have a sweet can, child. No wonder marshy Marshie wants to screw the bejesus out of it.''

"I have never had anal intercourse," said bent-over Joy haughtily.

"No but I mean the other way. Hell, you don't have to push back your pouch quite as much as that, darling."

"I can't help it. It's how I'm made. Oh, do get it over with, Vic, please."

"You're made to be fucked, screwed, rammed, stuck—and SPANKED!"

With which the lively brunette, her mini flipping, whacked the hard heel fully into the stretched seat of the right cheek.

"Ow," said the recipient softly.

The prefect waited a pause, then smacked it home again on the right. Each time the slipper struck it made a resonant slapping sound, completed with a little hiss of intaken breath or gasp from the bent girl, who was fleshy enough to still judder and jounce behind, even though partly bent over. She took five on the right, then five on the left.

"Warming up nicely?"

"It stings terribly, Vikki. Oh please only give me a few more."

Ten more whucked home on the right cheek now, so that by the last three the girl was slowly rising erect, her face twisted.

"Get right over, Joy. It can't hurt all that much."

"You don't know. It's absolute hell when you hit the same spot like that. Please, Vikki, let me off. I've been beaten enough."

"You haven't felt a thing. And in any case it was your own silly fault." The brunette was breathing in deeply herself by now. "Bend over and stick out your tushy."

Victoria hit as hard as she could into, this time, the left. She even drove her friend forward with the swat.

"Aow! Vikki, that's too hard!"

"No, that's nice, I like that." In reaction the slabby spheres had tried to clench in, thus imparting a vulnerable quiver to their insides and the insides of the mildly threshing thighs. "God, I wish I could get you another swiping from Miss Nicholson next half. You were made for beating, my sweet, and even I enjoy it. There! How's that for size. And . . . THAT!"

She finished in a flourish, whacking the heel hard inside the sensitive left cheek, and Joy grabbed herself, grimacing gorgeously. Victoria flung away the sandal, panting. She felt quickly under her skirt into her thick, closely furred furrow and found it panting, too. To think of school, and awful, hellish abstinence for another aching eight weeks. And to be caught with a dildo wasn't funny. The last girl to have one had hidden it in the hollow of a fake hockey stick, but it had been found, on one of the Duty Mistress' searches, and the offender had taken three dozen strokes of the birch in Great Hall, in full view of the whole school. A highly humiliating affair for a future Foreign Secretary's wife, being bent over buck-naked on a block while three mistresses gave a dozen each with twigs pickled in vinegar and wound in wire to lend them added toughness. The budded tips had bitten in the tender flesh either side the cringing cunt in a very beastly way indeed—as the recipient herself put it later, "They didn't have to hit me on the legs"—and altogether it was a rather somber audience that filed out of Great Hall after that salutory six minutes of excruciating sting across the most sensitive portions of an upper-class girl's most aristocratic anatomy. The whole thing was compounded by the fact that the sinner's parents, informed of her fault when the Head had requested permission to swipe their offspring, had asked that, to drive the lesson fully home, the birching be followed by six of the best with a cane each morning for a week—a reminder. After two such occasions, following the cold bath all Bothington girls took compulsorily of a morning, these canings became a very depressing prospect and the poor thing scarcely took her eyes off the floor for the rest of that week. No, it was too much of a bother bringing back a *godé*. If only that half-idiot milk roundsman was still there . . . .

Such memories, and others, occupied Victoria as she searched, swearing, around the room, one finger still stuck in her center.

"Oh Christ, what can I use?" She threw aside a girlish belt, too feeble by far. "All your things off, duckie, for the second half. This one's going to hurt."

"Which second half? Victoria, please." Joy was sitting on the silky satin bedspread of the bed—which was to say, on her hands on the bedspread. She squirmed her legs together. "What are you going to do now?" she almost wailed. But already she was meekly shedding her sweater; her bulleted boobs bounced on her torso. Like Victoria's superb pair they were tanned to their circular tips but, unlike her senior sister's, hers did not carry the white line of shoulder-strap Victoria primly affected. She thought it made them more sexy, but how you could improve The Bosom was a chimera of the gods themselves.

"God! Damn! And blast!" said Victoria, throwing things to the floor. She stormed into the bathroom, glared at their guillotined pantylegs, then said, "Ah! Just what the doctor ordered."

Naked Joy said. "No!" sharply.

"Come and get it," Victoria ordered, fuming, straddle-legged. "Perhaps this'll improve your memory, angel—from behind."

"No," said Joy. "Please. Not with that."

A plumber had visited them only that morning and absentmindedly enough, after he had shot his wad into the wettest twat he'd met on the Côte, had left some effects behind in a bucket, murmuring that he might be back on the morrow. Among these was a short strip of hard rubber hosing and this Victoria now brought down with all her weight on the painfully taut leather of a small pouffe, or hassock, before her. It even made a puff of dust.

*"No!"* gulped Joy.

"Don't be repetitive, dear. Get across here. Bottom up."

Nervously holding one hand over the cropped black snatch a-bulge beneath her belly (for Joy was no natural blonde), The Bottom came forward with a naturally nervous shudder.

"Please, Vic. That'll hurt like murder."

"Come on. You should have thought of that before being careless. Anyway, you know perfectly well you're all melty and toffeeish inside."

She was. Joy stood there, breast beating, like so much calendar art.

"How many?" she finally pouted.

"Five."

"Four."

"Six," said Victoria sternly. "And if you stall any more, my arithmetic goes crazy."

Joy draped herself forward over the hassock, head down. Her glorious ass, bisected by its buttery groove, was well reddened from its slippering. Indeed, closer inspection, such as that accorded it by Victoria now, would have revealed purplish contusions, in half-moons, where the heel had fallen and the nails there bitten. Victoria parted the globby masses a moment and looked into the great divide. The anal bud was adorably crinkled, and set rather deep within its amber crater, that so contrasted with the lily around.

"Six, just as hard as I know how," she got out through her teeth, "and let this be a lesson to you, minx."

So saying she swung—THUCKKK!

"*Gnao!*"

The tough rubber thumped in lustily, writing a wicked weal, and Joy stretched in pain. Victoria belted home the second, slap across the fat, and followed it quickly with a third. Joy yelped like a puppy, twisting.

"Christ! No . . . you don't know . . . stop, Vikki, please . . . hoooow it huuuuurts!"

She tried to get up and Victoria rapidly rapped in the last three with all her might, sending her comrade sprawling on the floor, where she writhed like some severed snake, moaning melodramatically.

"You der-didn't . . . darling . . . all that haaaaard," she breathed out in her agony.

But Victoria had ripped off her own garments, as if involved in some changing-room race, and now Joy found herself sprawling positively upwards, to bounce this time on the yielding mattress of the very French bed. The throw Victoria employed was a simple *ity-*

*hudi*, or bloater, and she eventually ended under the perspiring victim in a super sixty-nine. All tongues at once went to work. Directly Joy found hers she slipped it expertly into the creamy slit, wolfing the gristly morsel there, so that Victoria's thighs went taut and she arched, hissing, cursing with joy. Joy herself ardently sucked up the resultant liquor like so much soda pop, feeling fleshy lips now glued to her own . . . fleshy lips. Within her casket the pearl was now being most maddeningly wriggled and in a matter of moments it would, it would . . . she equally arched off the amazing swan's breast, whose nipples thumbed at her thighs, only to find her aching buttocks grabbed and drawn down and apart and . . . .

"Uuuuuuuu, sweetie, I think I'm going to . . . ."

Victoria stopped, possibly for breath. "You know, darling, I've had an idea."

"Oooooh, go ohhhhhnnnn, Vikki darling. Don't stop. I'm . . . ."

"A great idea."

"Suck, sweetheart. Lick. No, *suck*!"

"We're going on the streets. It's the only thing."

"LICKSUCKFRIIIII . . . I'm . . . going toooo . . . I'm . . . ."

"You *have*," said Victoria, with a creamy chuckle, half a minute (or a century) later. "What a deluge, you don't have to swamp me with it every time, Joy."

"I always do a lot."

"Especially after a good hiding, eh. You know it's twice as nice for you afterwards, isn't it?"

Joy didn't deny it. Just when the pain was receding it became perfect, poetic, paradisiacal. Muzzily she murmured, "What was that about . . . street-walking?"

"Just that you're going to do it, love. It's where the money's at."

"You serious, Vic?"

"Why not charge for putting it out?"

"But I like that . . . I mean, why me, why not you too?"

"All right, we'll work in shifts. First, we'll have to order orgies of condoms. Then we must change our room . . . ."

"We must change our town, darling," Joy perceived. "We're too well known right here."

"Right." Victoria snapped her idling fingers. "Move to Nice. More money."

"More men."

"With nice hard pricks."

They nuzzled into each happily, butting and bumbling, guzzling great gourds of flaccid flesh and giggling. Two healthy, happy, uninhibited English misses, who dearly wished to be rich.

# 4

"I'M GISY," SAID THE FIRST GIRL.

"I'm Jany," said the second.

"And I'm Maguy," said the third.

They barred the exit of the building into the sunny, sunny Rue France like so many birds of prey.

In her clingy little body dress of burgundy red Victoria Digby stared them out.

"I'm the Queen of Sheba," she said, and again attempted to push past them.

"This is our street."

"Only us work this street."

"Yeah. You two sows run home."

Victoria hit the middle one low in the belly and she doubled up, thus allowing The Bosom a dignified exit.

"Mémé fix you good," she heard a snarl behind, as she tick-tocked over to the café, or rather pizzeria, where The Bottom awaited her in a breathless hush. You could have heard a spoon drop as Victoria came in off the Nice street into the place. In a panic the Lithuanian waiter dropped a spoon.

"Have those three been bothering you again?" said

Joy, with a sumptuous sigh. She wore a coal-blue knit minislink with a lowslung grosgrain belt. "They went at me yesterday like cats. Who are they? Or, rather, who do they think they are?"

"Seem to think they own the place," said Victoria, sipping her chum's mint tea. "Maybe they do. Now off you go, ffrench, and french. I've done my sting for the day and I'm proud to say," she patted her purse, "we're running nicely ahead. A few more clients like that and I think we can call it a day."

"Who," said Joy timidly, the saucers of her violet eyes dropping to her saucer, "what . . . did you get this time?"

"Another damn bagpiper," ticked Victoria crossly. "And he had to spurt in my face, too." She riffled her gourds together in memory; the man, an Italian construction worker, had been loaded, so she had let him put his cheerfully gnarled cock to nuzzle in the valley of her bosom, The Bosom, which she had first anointed with suntan oil. The grinning oaf had handled the slippery surfaces like this waiter was handling his dishes, rapturously shagging himself astraddle the waves of her belly while she lay back panting. Finally he had shot off before she was ready with a towel, spurting into her cursing face, and jabbering in Abruzzi. "There are times when one has to draw the line," she said pensively now. "Spitting in a lady's eye, for instance. So far my score up the cunt is nil. It's either been bagpiping or frenching, and mostly the former. Oh well." And she patted her well-pouched purse again. It was their third day in Nice and their second of sin. Street-walking had really proved laughably easy. There was nothing to it. "Now get over there and get cracking," she instructed dimpling Joy. "And by cracking I mean cracking."

"Isn't that?" said Joy, standing up. "I mean that's the man Marshall . . . ."

"By Golly, the good old Argentinian," Victoria jumped up, sending things crashing around and this time the waiter dropped the whole tray. "Wait till I get my hands on *him*!"

"Vikki, I don't think I care to . . . ."

"Oil wells and steel mills and . . . ."

"I will not be buggered," said Joy primly as her senior in sin, as in other things, made a dexterous dart across the street, intercepting the tanned, wrinkled millionaire with his mock-turtle face before the beady three could offer their wares first. It was a resolute confrontation for a matter of minutes and then the smiling Argentinian shadowed off into the alleyway leading to their room, The Room. Joy found herself beckoned over.

"Josito remembers you. Er, it," corrected Victoria sternly. "From Ste. Maxime."

"No," said Joy softly.

"He wants to beat you."

"No," said Joy loudly.

"On The Bottom. I'll be there to supervize, and see it's not too hard. I mean, not too really hard. Five hundred francs."

"But, but . . . ."

"And if he wants to stuff it up your itchy little twat afterwards it's another five hundred."

"But I've only just been beaten," came the weak wail.

"Nonsense. A mere nothing. Those marks have almost gone. Think of it. Five hundred filthy francs, luv. Come on."

"Well, only if you do it, Vic."

"All right."

Josito, the wise Argentinian, chose politely to follow the two full fannies, under their flirty skirts, as they threaded amicably up the four flights to The Room. He could have continued up that staircase for ever. The way that blonde's sulcus fatted in and out . . . out and in . . . .

"What are you doing here?"

Raven-haired Victoria eyeball-to-eyeballed tense, equally inky-locked little Gisy, who stood barring their path to The room, her legs like rapiers under the skinny mini.

"No one works our street. Only us."

It was all she could say. Victoria sent her sprawling halfway down the flight with a well-timed *moboku;* the whore lay spitting and snarling, trying to sort out the stars, as Victoria opened the door—"After you, Josito."

It had been hard to get a room in Nice. Or a bed. For the two in this case were the same. Once in The Room you were in The Bed. Which was to say, when you were in The Bed you were in The Room. It was a perfect syllogism. And a very big bed.

"Buck naked," Victoria snapped, scenting excitement as they entered. "On The bed. On your belly, dearie."

"What are you going to do it with?" mumbled Joy, starting to shed.

The Argentinian took off his white silk shirt. He had a lean sinewy brown body that gave both girls pause at once; the man really wasn't bad-looking at all. Only his face was wrinkled. His body was twenty-five, a very strong twenty-five indeed. Victoria eyed the visible masthead of his prick, under the white silk trousers. She proffered a slipper. He shook his head. A belt.

"Too soft. I show you. Look."

He opened a wall, which was to say their closet, extracted a wire hanger and, before Joy's shuddering gaze, bent it straight—into a single line of agonizing steel, very thin, very whippy—with his immensely powerful hands.

"I see what you mean," said Victoria, taking it respectfully.

Naked Joy objected abjectly—"Vikki! You can't. Not with that. It'll cut me in half. Please."

"It will hurt," Victoria said meditatively.

"It'll make me bleed."

"With your legs together and the pillow under your pelvis," coaxed the turtle gently.

"Vikki!"

"I don't think it'll do her any harm, do you?" The older girl turned to her client. "All the same, it will be somewhat severe. You did say five hundred, didn't you?" Her eyes gimleted. "Five hundred what, mister? Francs or dollars?"

"What does it matter?" grinned the man in reply, taking a billfold from his pocket and tossing U.S. twenty-spots around like so much confetti. Victoria looked at them descending with considerable respect. "Pounds if you like."

"I like," said Victoria. She was starting to seethe nicely inside. The sight of The Bottom always did it to her. She might as well enjoy it, after all. That way it was much more personal. "Lie like he told you, worm," she hissed imperiously. "Stick that fat tushy up and don't pretend you aren't feeling all squidgy inside."

"How many?" gasped Joy, adjusting the pillow under her tuft.

Josito answered slowly—"Since it won't be a male arm, I think it should be at least a dozen."

"Please."

"Or like, fifteen," agreed Victoria licking her chops. "If you could make those pounds . . . ."

"I could," said Josito. And did.

"That's a very serious sum of money," said Victoria.

"That's a very serious *Sitzplatz*," said Josito. "The finest I have ever seen. Hit it here." A sepia fingernail traced above the sulcus, where the flesh was lightly mottled by the marblings of the previous "swiping". "Just above the tan line."

"And right behind her we-know-what. Stretch out, scum, and keep it there. It'll be extra if you move."

Victoria, breathing deeply, was entering into the spirit of things. As she tapped the huddling rump in aim (noticing how Joy had wadded the counterpane into her mouth) she began to feel the sun behind her eyes.

The man gave her a gently tap. "Would you mind divesting yourself of your raiment while you do this?"

"Why, I'd be delighted, Count." She pirouetted politely and started unfastening. "I'll just keep my bra on, if you don't mind. My bubbies do bounce around so when I give a beating." Naked but for it she returned to her ardent task.

"That's a magnificent bush you have."

"Thank you, kind sir." She dipped in best Bothington curtsey.

"What a cunt. May I? This clitoris . . . why, it's . . . ."

Victoria stood astride. "Big as a boy's little finger, they tell me. Though it's usually his index one . . . hou, ouch, hey!"

"Is it always as large as this?"

"When I'm going to ber-beat Joy it is!"

"May I examine it from the rear?"

"For five hundred pounds you can . . . ram it . . . from the rear . . . and as a matter of fact, I wer-wish you w-w-w- . . . ."

The words ended on a tiny stifled scream. It had happened so fast. She had been decently bending over for him to see her pride, that pink slotted fig at the bisection of her butties, when suddenly he had slucked into her.

The penetration of quite the largest prick she had ever felt straightened her a second, then suddenly she was pounding at him, a-tiptoe, fighting to unskewer herself from this ramrod. For her entrails told her not only of its immense girth, but that there were several more inches to come. Christ!

"No . . . nugh . . . no!"

She toppled on The Bed, crashing softly into Joy, and more of the prick ploughed slickly into her as the man continued to impale her there. Indeed, those wiry brown hands tore off her bra and twisted her nipples till she screamed. Or would have, and had her face not been muffled in snatch, Joy having turned over beneath her and jammed her crotch at her mouth.

"Nnngggh . . . ough . . . pffff!"

Fighting to get free, she was screwed from behind while Joy frantically frigged herself on her chin. She felt breathless, full up; grunting, snorting and sweating in positive bursts she tried to worm forward over all the limbs and loins—"Goddamnit, you'll kill me with that thing!"—when volted lightning struck her guts. She became sheer cunt. She rode up, pumping and suctioning, felt the jam of balls at her belly as she bucked, then jacked like a breathless bow while he scalded off into her, in jets that seemed to thrash her throat. At last she collapsed, mushy. She never felt him slide out of her. Or even heard him leave the room. Josito moved gently, a careful cat.

Aeons later she was aware of Joy jamming closer, hugging.

"I never even came," she heard in a discontented voice. She tried to put her scalp back on.

"Jesus, what a fuck. That bastard practically pulled my nipples off, you know it. Agony."

"You could have made me come," said Joy, butting her furry mound into one thigh.

"Darling, about all I was conscious of was cock. I could scarcely breathe. For a second I thought I was going to be sick. He reamed me to the eyeballs. Wow!"

"I know. I squirmed round and got my face right under your cunt."

"That was your chin down there, was it."

"His balls kept hitting my nose. I wanted to sneeze. But the way your lips opened and closed as it went in and out . . . ."

"It was enormous, wasn't it?"

"Ooooh." The girl gave a little thrilled ripple. "A murderous engine, if ever there was one."

"Well, I was plugged all right. I've never felt so fucked in my life before."

"Vikki, do you think you could . . . if I get like this . . . it was so exciting seeing you and all. And I was so frightened about being whipped."

"I'll bet you creamed three times. Go and shut the door first, you brazen hussy."

But a man was standing in the door. A man with gold teeth.

"Fucky-fucky?" he was saying.

The girls grabbed at clothes and sheets.

"I don't believe we've had the pleasure of being introduced," said Victoria icily, sitting up and feeling come stream out of her in a steady ooze.

"Fucky-fucky," said the man, smiling.

"Get out," commanded Joy.

"Fucky-fucky."

"You must be kidding," Victoria said in her most hostile tone. "I couldn't go another for all the tea in China. And I do mean tea. Anyhow," she said with a startled look at the snow of notes around, "I believe we're adequately provided for at present. At least for another four or five years, shall we say."

"Nice house . . . Antibes . . . you come," said the grinning gargoyle in the doorway. "Nice man . . . you come . . . Antibes . . . big villa . . . much money . . . you come."

"Thanks, I just came," said Victoria coldly. "Now get lost."

But the man stood there. "You come," he said.

"You already said that."

"You come." And this time the man with gold teeth was holding a gun.

# 5

GOLD TEETH DROVE LIKE AN EXPERT IN HANdling wheels.

Which was to say, roulette wheels.

He slid the open Buick in and out the early evening traffic on the Coast road out of Nice with grinning aplomb, as well as, so increasingly apprehensive Victoria observed, a constant erection. They should never have taken on the assignment in the first place—they had all the bread they needed now—but there hadn't been all that alternative, not with that blue-eyed Beretta about. And then Joy had given her most plaintive look—"Just this last one, Vic. I'm dying for a fuck."

"Oh shit, and here I am streaming goo." Victoria had swung her aristocratic limbs over the side of The Bed. "All right, you"—eyeing Gold Teeth—"wait in the hallway. We'll be out in a jiff."

Twenty minutes, and five eye-shades each, later they had been, herself in bell bottoms and a blouse of panné velvet, Joy in a skimpy little pull-on knit of golden nugget wool, with a U-patch pocket and big buckled belt, completing the ensemble with a silly cloche hat and cowhide bag.

"Beauty and The Bust," she had announced to Gold Teeth, with a mocking bow.

Now, sitting next to him in the open Buick, she felt, yes, much less sure of herself. There was no call for this colossal erection; her brown bell bottoms hugged her hips closely, but there was no legwork on display. Or was it simply the proximity of The Bosom? She was rapidly regretting the whole thing.

"Where is this place?"

They were close to the sea in a wooded area now, a district of marshmallow villas sprawling under elegant elms. Suddenly Gold Teeth pointed and swung down a track. There was a large grilled gate with Villa Merenda on the top. There were also two enormous dogs. The gate opened by itself, and closed with a blue-chip, photo-electric snuck behind them. Joy whispered, "Wow!" as they cruised down a gravel drive with vistas of shimmering sea and a little private jetty below. Gold Teeth pulled up at the main house, a low white villa reeking of elegance. Both girls stilt-heeled in, with becomingly distant expressions on their faces. They were shown into a long calcined room, very comfortably furnished with Arab-type cushions and throw rugs, and expensive leather chairs.

"If you would wait . . ." Gold Teeth grinned. "My boss see you soon."

Victoria nodded . . . distantly.

Joy was whistling in front of a picture. "Hey, isn't this a Picasso?"

"And this a Degas. Our price has gone up already, dearie."

"I'll let you handle that end of it, Vikki," said the younger, frowning. "You're so good at figures."

"Chiefly yours."

After a while Gold Teeth came back, bowed.

"The presence of Mademoiselle," and he indicated Joy, "is required."

"We go together," said Victoria defensively.

Gold Teeth smiled slowly.

"Okay," Victoria said with a shiver, "only don't keep me waiting too long."

When Joy had gone out she slumped in a low seat with some old copies of *Vogue* and *Elle*. She was growing more and more uncomfortable. She was certain she was being watched in some manner. She got up, sat down. Ran a hand over the snug fit of her slacks.

"Very nice," said a man's voice appreciatively. She spun. There was no one there. She was growing definitely frightened. "Now, if you would be so good, Mademoiselle, and take the spiral staircase at the end of the room—no, in that direction there—and descend to the bottom of it." She moved, bemused, and the voice moved amusedly with her. "Another flight . . . a little dark . . . but turn to your right . . . ."

At the foot of the white-plastered stair was some hallway or room, she couldn't tell which, it was almost pitch dark. She felt her way forward, groping.

Suddenly she gave a long hissing cry, and grabbed back with both hands, whirling. She had just been given an absolutely excruciating stroke across her noble posteriors.

"Get in there!"

Still panting with pain she was thrust out of the darkness through a suddenly opened door. Into a big bare room. The light there dazzled her. Still staggering with the agony of that soulless slice about her bum she turned and saw Gold Teeth closing the door behind her; he had a murderous cravache or quirt in his right hand. She nursed herself sorely, trying to think of something crushing to say to him when a thickly accented voice said, "Not a very ladylike entry, Miss Digby, but I think you know everyone present."

It was the voice she had been guided down by and it came from a small man—really little more than a dwarf—with much curly oily black hair, seated behind a refectory table at the far end. Then all at once her gaze sharpened. Three women were standing near him. Gisy . . . Jany . . . Maguy.

"I don't believe . . . ." Victoria automatically began, when she broke off. She was really feeling very scared.

Little ink-locked Gisy came forward first, her foxy muzzle of a face beaming.

"Remember me, bitch?" she said, standing in front of Victoria in her short sleek mini. And she slogged the English girl in the side, just above the solar plexus, with her fist.

Victoria doubled, breathless, mouth open, and received a crashing blow in the face. As she went down Gisy kicked her with all her strength in the crotch. On her knees, head hung, Victoria yelped like a beaten puppy. The man shouted out something in a bizarre, guttural tongue to the woman, but Gisy got two more ringing cracks to Victoria's aching head before Gold Teeth pulled her off.

"Stand up," he said, "in front of the boss."

What was that? Victoria shook her muddled mind. Standing up? On all fours she fought for something called breath. That was all that mattered for the moment.

*Thththwwshhh!*

The air she sought whickered and her eyes danced out of her head and back, as the cravache soughed into her buttocks again, ferociously, spasming her in pain and arching her up. Frantically rubbing she rose to her feet.

"You didn't have to do that," she said to Gold

Teeth. "What's all this in aid of, anyway? Where's Joy? Jesus Christ, that hurt."

Maguy, the tallest and also brunette, minced forward menacingly.

"Listen, sow, by the time Mémé finished with you, you'll wish you ain't been born with no fat backside. He teach you a lesson, good. Those big boobs—you ever seen a pair of nipples after they been fried? He mark you for life." She spat, copiously, in Victoria's face and withdrew.

It was Jany's turn. She was a plump, cheerful-looking blonde. "Mémé trains Arab ponies with that cravache. He train you good, too. After half a dozen you be crawling up the walk, cow. Another six and you'll beg to eat shit." She paused, reflectively. "Come to think of it, I could. You ever tasted shit, cow?"

Victoria disdained to answer; she remembered Helen Elstir most distinctly, but a Bothington behind . . . in comparison with these witches.

"Give her another," said Gisy.

"Two," added Maguy.

"Touch your toes," said Jany.

'No," cried Victoria, seeing Gold Teeth backing off for aim. "What is this? What do you want to know?"

"Who you work for," said the dwarf crisply then.

"What do you mean?"

"Rue France is mine," he said.

Suddenly Victoria had it. She wanted to laugh hysterically. Of course. This was the pimp, the famous *maquereau* of French legend, the fish that fed on other fish, and his broads were spitting mad. That street was their turf. She spilt out their story quickly and gladly.

"Now that little misunderstand's straightened out," she said in the silence that followed her summary account of their summery follies, and keeping a wary eye on that greedy whipcord tail of the long cravache behind her.

The silence persisted. Finally the little man said, "Bend over and touch your toes."

Striving to keep some sensible upper-class British command in the air, Victoria said, "It isn't necessary, really."

"All the same I'd prefer you to do it."

"I never was too good at touching my toes."

"Have done with it, Mémé," called one of the harpies, "tie her up and give her a dozen. I want to see that backside bleed."

"What I told you was the truth."

"It ties in with what your friend told me, yes. And with your papers, too. But I don't believe you. There just aren't any more independents left on the Côte . . . ."

"They all seem to end up with their throats slit," sneered Maguy sullenly.

"Or with lead weights round their legs," chimed in Jany. She gestured. "There's an awful lot of sea out there."

"You must be working for someone. Sauveur . . . or that Spaniard Ramon . . . in Marseilles . . . ."

"I swear it's the truth."

The dark pimp shrugged. "I'm going to have to flog you."

"I shall have to see the Ambassador."

"I shall flog you and return you to your father when I know your *cäid*."

"My father is an Ambassador," said Victoria icily. "He also happens to be an Earl."

There were guffaws from the girls at this information.

Victoria suddenly felt she wanted to cry.

"Bend over. You'll find it does its work much better bent tight. Best Corsican boar's hide."

"I j-just don't want another one . . . with that wh-whip."

But she got it. The air thrummed and the tapering rapier sliced right through her seat again, jacking her straight and making her stamp speechless with pain as its sting continued to worry and burrow right into her. She puffed and rubbed to the delight of the applauding hookers.

"Now I'll show you your school chum," said Mémé the pimp, and he got up and went to the door.

It led to a room that smelt of pain. The Bothington gym was cherry by comparison. One wall was hung with whips and straps. There were pulleys on another. Trestles and benches to one side. Rue-faced Victoria trooped in, still rubbing, in front of the smiling whores.

"Joy!" she exclaimed.

At first sight her friend did not appear in any unusual trouble. She was seated on a small steel typing stool, it seemed. True, her arms were held tight behind her, in leather cuffs that caught each wrist to its opposing elbow; and true, her legs were crossed at ankles and fettered to the seat below. Still, she had on her clothes. She even still wore the silly cloche hat.

"Please, Vikki, please," came from the curiously woebegone face which not only looked about to cry, it looked as if it had cried a lot already. "Please tell him we did this on our own . . . he wouldn't believe me . . . and God how it hurts."

"What does?" said Victoria.

"See for yourself," grinned the dwarf. "This is one we got from the OAS. They even say some of those Arab twitches liked it."

Joy was ooohing and aaahing, turning her face this way and that, her breasts thrusting, her mouth wide. Victoria noted that like a good Bothington girl she had not sat on her skirt, but on the seat. Tentatively she lifted the golden glad lap-rag behind. The seat was shaped like a saddle, thus widely parting the magnificently beveled contours of The Bottom. They had taken off her panties. The thighs were trying arduously to gain some leverage on the frontal plates to raise that most darling derrière up a fraction. For the mighty arse-cheeks were spread to distension by the penetration of a monstrous meatus up the anus, also made of steel, slightly serrated and now a little greasy. It was affixed to the steel seat most stoutly.

"She should have it up the cunt," cried Gisy. "Hurts more than in the arsehole."

"Even so it made her jump a bit," said Maguy, "you must admit."

"When she got that shot of hot oil, it almost spouted out of her nostrils," said Jany. "Just as well this room is soundproof."

"Turn it on," said the pimp.

"NAOOOHHH!" screamed Joy tensely.

"That's a rotten thing to do to a girl," said Victoria worriedly. This was really happening, yet.

The small man said, "Such noises. We have all the latest gadgets here."

"Not the one that goes up cunt and arse, both," said Gisy.

He frowned. "It's on order. Look," he turned to Victoria. "Ever had an electrical scalp treatment?"

"I don't believe I have," Victoria said, more faintly.

"I turn this knob to ten . . . ."

"To twenty," said Jany.

"Thirty," bidded Maguy.

"NAOOOOOOOH!" wailed Joy, vainly trying to jump.

The knob at the back of the chair-strut was turned, and the girl started moving and moaning on her seat and prick.

"Oooh . . . ow . . . uuuuh . . . it's so . . . ough!"

"Feel the plates," gently invited the smiling pimp. "With the current running through them at ten it's no more than a rather sharp prickling sensation, a sort of pins and needles on thighs and ass, not to mention up that lovely supple tunnel . . . and when I turn to fifteen . . . ."

"NOOOOOOOH!" shouted Joy.

Victoria snatched her hand away. The steel was giving off a rapping stabbing sensation, like tiny daggers on the skin. What it must be like up the . . . but Joy's eyes were rolling like those of a driven beast. Her mouth gaped wide, gasping.

"There's one model that heats up nicely, too," said the dwarf. "And another that plunges. But even with my own private jetty, shipping restrictions . . . ."

Victoria said, "Our story's true. You won't get anything out of her, I swear. We're sorry."

"Be sorrier in a minute," said Gisy.

"Put it up to thirty, Mémé, and have done with the slut."

The pimp approached. Slowly he fondled the dial. Joy's eyes went quite wild.

"Nooooo . . . no more . . . stop him, Vikki, pleeeeeazzze!"

"One shot then, sweetheart," said the dwarf gently, "just to let you know what this thing can really do. And don't forget the grab off a slice of the sun for me, as you go sailing by." He flicked up the knob and held it there a second.

The effect was, in every sense, electrical. With a strangled squeal Joy stiffened hideously, lifting herself as far off the chair as her bonds would permit. Under the uplifted tail of stuff behind Victoria saw the buttocks clench desperately up off the frightful pulsing metal prick; in this pose the dwarf held her his steady second, as she tried to lose more of the awful anal penetration, then slumped her back exhausted, making gargling sound in her throat, as the current was cut off.

"That's what I call a shot up the ass," said Gisy as Gold Teeth unbound the half-conscious girl. "One up the twat would teach her to be so greedy with her stuff, too."

"I still say," said Victoria, though she did so in a whisper, "that's a rotten, rotten thing to do to a girl."

"Now let's give this one a try."

"It isn't necessary," said Victoria. She was in a mad admixture of emotions, half crazy, futile fear, and half rabid excitement at the sight of Joy, sitting with panties restored and order in her dress slugging some brandy Gold Teeth had given her. "We've told the truth and that's all there is."

Oddly, the dwarf seemed to be losing interest in the proceedings, fiddling with some switches and pulling out a screwdriver.

"The wiring that guy put in is lousy, I said so from the start."

"I . . . I . . . ." Joy was standing, tears welling from her very violet eyes, her cloche hat only slightly awry.

"Yeah, Jany, better take Mademoiselle to the john." He gave Victoria his best leer. "They always want to, after a shot."

"Come with me, pretty." But taking Joy's hand, something made Jany pause. She raised the pan of skirt and peeked into the panties. "Dear me. This one already has."

"I couldn't help it," sobbed Joy.

"I'll have to give you a spanking for that, my pet. Now come on and follow *maman*."

Victoria was only too aware that things in the room were not turning out well for her.

"Welcome to the Villa Merenda," said Maguy, picking up the quirt.

"Take them down, cunt, and then take them right off," said Gisy.

Victoria looked around. The dwarf was fiddling with his switches, unscrewing some screw. Gold Teeth was taking off his jacket and putting his armpit holster on a table. She felt she was losing the battle. Her fingers were feeling for her zip.

"Don't whip me with that thing, please."

"The blouse as well. Let's see those knockers, dearie."

*"Tiens!"*

"How many, boss?"

*"Please!"*

She really was now in shameful, scalding tears. After all she was only seventeen.

"Oh give her a dozen." From the dwarf, crouched by a wall plug, cursing.

"A dozen? Ter-twelve! But I've had three already."

Victoria turned hectically around.

"Please."

"Eat shit," said Gisy. "Remember?"

"Drink piss," said Maguy lugubriously.

She would do anything, anything, to avoid the touch of the tapering stretch of hide with its awful, awful, breathtaking cord trainer that stung so on the right. But the two streetwalkers were tenderly taking her arms.

They led her to a trestle, a horrible saw-horse.

"You don't have to . . ." she began, to break off in a blubber. Yes, she was crying like a child. It wasn't fair. There were three burning bars across her backside, and she didn't want any more. "Please don't whip me any more. I'll do anything you say."

"Anything, she says," said Gisy, cocking a pincered eyebrow.

"Let's have some fun with her first," said tall Maguy, clapping her hands. "Let's, let's."

"Ever been syringed up the cunt with hot chile water, sow?" asked Gisy from one side.

"Or had a horse suppository up the anus?" said Maguy from the other. "The kind that makes them stick their tails up straight."

"And makes little girls want to turn their entrails inside out."

"What about the bar?"

"The swing!"

"The pin-cushion!"

"Human, of course. The bicycle!"

"Only thing is, it doesn't have a saddle."

"That's the hell of it, I'm afraid."

"The bicycle is out of order," said the dwarf, from the floor.

"Singe off her bush."

"Snip off a nipple. Just one."

"Stand up," said Gisy.

"Sit down," said Maguy.

"I'll do anything, anything you say," whimpered Victoria ignominiously, as she obeyed.

"Do you hear that, Gisy? I do believe she will."

"Maybe she's even ready to eat shit."

"Drink piss."

"Let's see."

"Will you let me off if I do?" moaned Victoria miserably.

"What a bargainer! We'll see how well you do it, first. On your knees, bitch. Gisy dear, do you have a bonbon left?"

"Certainly."

It was unwrapped from the tiny lizard-skin purse, a large dark lozenge. Maguy reached under her skirt—

both girls appeared to be pantyless for the fray—and, an absent expression on her face, pushed it up behind.

"Just coat it with chocolate for you, first."

Meanwhile, sleek-headed Gisy, not to be outdone, returned from the side with a glass. She held it under her skirt, and tinkled prettily.

"Damn," she said as she drew the amber goblet forth, "thought I could go a bit more than that."

"That sherry's not even frothy," said Maguy. She did an agile squat and pinged her coated lozenge on the floor. "Now. Pick it up in your mouth, swine, chew it and see how sweet French shit can taste. Afterwards, Gisy will give you your little apéritif."

"Afterwards I take her ass off," said Gold Teeth, who had grown impatient.

"Only slowly," said Gisy.

After it was done, and Victoria had swallowed her bitter draught, she was strapped to a trestle. She had given up all hope and lay over it, sniffling, while the two women secured her. They did so soundly.

She was most utterly, completely and sexily arse up, her legs widespread and attached to the struts one end, while her upper body was fastened by a waist-belt to the central limb of the thing. This inclined sharply downwards, so that her head was lower than her crotch and she saw everything upside down. Like, for instance, Gold Teeth's pointed perforated shoes as he retreated a safe distance to take aim. Like the terrible tail of that cravache. Her wrists were buckled to cuffs in the waist-belt in back.

"A real English cunt," said Gisy. "Mmn. Fat and shaggy."

"Also," remarked Maguy, "wet. They do say they like it over there."

"Beat the shit out of her."

"Only, slowly."

Victoria set herself. If she was to get it she was to get it. Let them see how a Bothington Prefect could take a beating. She tried to tighten up her cheeks a little to avoid excessive exposure.

"Twelve."

"Slowly."

PPHHHRWUPPP!

There was that sad sound in the air of suddenly riven fabric, then the shock of white-hot coals searing the most tender skin of her bum. She grunted, lunging. The brute. He had cut low down. School experience had taught her that the worse pain came ten seconds later and she clenched her teeth to fight it, bitterly. It was rending, furious agony. She felt her right cheek involuntarily cringing from the tip.

Maguy was fondling her right dug, hanging one side the central strut, and Gisy the other.

"Cheer up, sow," said the latter, "only eleven more now."

"Only a little harder."

THHHRWUPPP!

*"Christ!"*

The second was very much worse; the lash wound round her and the trainer seemed to pause, then flick in with venom. He was cutting so damn skilfully, she knew. After the third they gave her a long pause. She was panting like some surfacing diver.

"She's beginning to look better from behind, Maguy."

"It's the Union Jack, the Union Jack."

"You might at least," she gasped, "please . . . come up a little higher." Her cunt seemed to be quaking in her center.

Suddenly she heard the man say something in a guttural growl. It was that Italian-sounding dialect again. Whatever he said, it annoyed the whores. Who answered him in kind. Invective flew over Victoria's broad rump like hail.

Nine more, she couldn't conceivably stand nine more.

All at once, between her legs, she saw the upside-down shaft of Gold Teeth's animal prick sprouting from his trousers. It came cleaving the air towards her while the two girls swore at him in Corse.

She realized in a flash that this would end her agony. She couldn't possibly get to twelve, and if only . . . .

"Please, please," she heard herself begging, imploring.

"Such noise," called the dwarf from the floor, a row of nails in one side of his mouth.

"Take me . . . screw me . . . have me . . . anything . . . bugger me, only for God's sake don't beat me any more."

It was, in the French saying, exact. The Cyclops eye in the gaunt mushroom head of the thing nuzzled puppylike at her quim, salivating itself there a second, then Victoria felt twin thumbs pressed either side her anal hole, opening it out like a fruit. The girls gave up their snarling and watched, giving practical instructions.

"Just an inch first, then jam it right up her."

"Let her feel it to the eyeballs."

"That's the sphincter-ring, *mon vieux*. Once through that you're home."

"You're home," clapped Maguy ecstatically.

"NNNNNGH!" grunted Victoria as the rock-hard prick slipped up the tallow of her entrails. It was much worse than she'd expected, more filling and frightening, and it was very much worse than that still when he began heartlessly to piston in and out of her. Ye Gods, the man was using her guts as a glove. She began to groan and sweat. "Please . . . ow . . . oh God . . . shoot it in soon . . . please."

"The slut is begging for it now."

"I knew she would."

"How does it feel to have nine inches of Corsican gristle up your backside, slut?"

The two heads were close to hers and kept up their Greek chorus of raillery and abuse until the man came inside her in seething gusts of squirting semen. Victoria wondered whether she was going to vomit. But she had got out of her beating, thank God. Here were the two twitches unstrapping her. After the scene on the trestle Gisy and Maguy seemed to have altered their attitude. Gold Teeth didn't even trouble to do up his fly. Victoria made in as dignified a manner as she might for her trousers, which she donned after first wiping herself with a Malines lace handkerchief not much larger than a postage stamp.

"Now, if you people have quite finished, I'd be grateful to be allowed to leave."

From the floor the dwarf barked out, "I don't believe this moron even knew our voltage here." He stared disconsolately at what looked like the small parts of a motor bicycle lying strewn in front of him.

"I'll show you to your room, dear," said Maguy sweetly, and she proceeded to do so, leading Victoria by the hand. Her manner had indeed totally changed.

In a passage Victoria said, "I want to go."

"There's a W.C. in the bathroom, dear."

"No. I mean split. Vamoose. Get the hell out of here."

"In the morning, *chérie*."

Victoria had had enough of this female Mutt and Jeff couple. She wasn't fooling with Maguy any more. Maguy, meanwhile, was feeling over the curves of Victoria's wounded can. The trousers clung real close.

"You have a lovely derrière, dear."

"It's usually the top-deck they admire. Ouch. That's where he . . . ."

"Well I love your adorable, well-fed British bottom," said Maguy smiling. "It was just beginning to wriggle nicely, too. First time you've been buggered?"

"Actually, yes."

"Nice?"

"Quite utterly disgusting."

"I never let clients do it to me. At least not for under a hundred. But you . . . maybe in the morning you and I . . ." She paused before a door. In her sweetest tone of voice she said, "I will conclude by warning you of the necessity of your absolutely complete obedience to all rules at the Villa Merenda."

"That goes without saying," said Victoria with a shiver.

"Mémé hates people breaking rules. I do regret all this happened, but he will look after you in the morning. It could be worse."

"Not with that riding quirt it couldn't," said Victoria.

"May I warn you that the bedroom will be thoroughly locked as to windows and doors, thus denying all egress, but that after a light supper had been brought up to you both, the floor will be given current. It would be uncomfortable to step out of bed. I suggest you use the bathroom beforehand. Bed-pans are at both sides of the bed for urgent needs at night. The room is completely wired and also monitored with a seeing eye. Sleep tight, *chérie*."

So saying, Maguy opened the door, gave Victoria a pecking kiss on the cheek, who passed through to hear a key turn in the lock behind her.

"Look who's here," she said. "Mrs. Livingstone, I presume."

Joy was lying under the pink silk sheets of a mammoth bed in quite the fanciest bedroom even Victoria

Digby had ever seen. Its view over the final firs of the coast and the blue wavelets of the Mediterranean was an invitation to romance itself. The house was cradled in a creek, admiring itself in the mirror of a lavish pool of lightly rocking green water far beneath.

Joy sat up straight, her quick blonde tow swinging with her bare boobs, her face more heart-shaped and beautifully forlorn than ever.

"Vikki, darling. What did they do to you? Did they whip you? Was it . . . awful?"

"What do you think?" Victoria turned and eased off her pants in a single lithe movement. She needed to go to the bathroom.

"Ooooh."

"I got three of the most excruciatingly painful strokes imaginable with that whip thing across my beautiful bottom. Or rather, the base of it, where it joins the thighs. I never thought a stroke could be so painful. I can still feel each one ringing behind my ears. After which," she completed, folding up her blouselet, "that bastard chose to bugger me."

"Oooh. Vikki. Like me."

"Yes you were, in a way, weren't you. That pole up your ass must have been hell."

"It was hideous. And then that, that woman kercaned me. For incontinence. And it wasn't my fault. Look."

The pouting blonde nymphet knelt, showing her bottom, The Bottom, in a parody of pin-up art. Six velvety black lines had been inscribed across it. Victoria felt a sudden roaring eruption of gismic desire in her loins. She hurried in to the bathroom, to sit.

When she had completed her ablutions she hastened, naked, into the bed beside Joy.

"I wish Aunt Grizel were here," said Joy. "What are they going to do with us, do you think?"

"Play up School," said Victoria, snuggling.
"Play up School," echoed Joy dubiously.
They huddled together in each other's arms. Perhaps, after all, things might have been worse.
The blank screen monitoring their movements from the ceiling seemed to think so, at any rate.

# 6

"**D**O YOU HAVE A TENNIS COURT HERE?"

"No but I can beat you at swimming. Want to try?"

At the word *beat* Victoria's pensive eyes flicked to their host. It was ten o'clock the following morning and she and Joy were sipping café-au-lait spiked with a spot of cointreau on the gloriously sunny sea terrace of the Villa Merenda, overlooking the private jetty. A yacht was tied up, and some bronzed men were unloading things and carrying them up a piney path. It was a sleepy day. Sunny.

"I still say," said Victoria emphatically, "that was a rotten thing to do to a girl."

She looked at Joy, stretching her lissom legs on a canvas seat the other side of the smiling dwarf. Her companion in disaster looked scrumptious today in a slithery little white matte jersey thing with a surplice neckline and a lightly gathered skirt. Perfect for sun country. Could be folded in an envelope, and frequently was. The dwarf was in a toweling robe and she herself had on an absurd mint green bikini, wet but drying fast in the sun. She sighed deeply and her pride prodded at the sodden stuff with twin bullets. A cold dip always made her nips stand out. Wasn't it said that burley dancers iced them? All the same . . . .

"Mémé Pizziani never forgets a debt," said the dark dwarf expansively. He had on swim trunks and a short shirt.

Victoria pasted her succulent croissant with best Chivers' marmelade and masticated slowly and luxuriously, twiddling her bare toes on the seat-rest. Her eyes contemplated the veritable brick of piled-high bank notes lying on the napery of the table before her. Bank of England notes.

"Did you say all of those are ponies?" she inquired solicitously. "Twenty-spots?"

The dwarf tutted, shocked. "All fifty-pound notes, my friend."

"Really." She bent forward and inspected. "I didn't know there were such things. Did you make them this morning or something?"

The dwarf chuckled. "Non-serial numbers. You can go into any bank in Cannes and deposit those. With my chauffeur now, if you wish."

Riffling, Victoria reflected. "If your chauffeur is the one with gold teeth, I'll pass that one up, Mémé, if you don't mind. He drives with a constant erection."

"He does everything with a constant erection. A good hard prick."

"I'll say. You seem to forget I felt it in an intimate region yesterday evening. Jesus Christ, I do believe there are two thousand pounds here."

"I hope you'll accept the compensation," said the dwarf amicably. "And let bygones be bygones. It was a mistake, but I was convinced you were working for Ramon."

"Joy, what do you think?"

"I leave it to you, Vikki."

"She's tired, poor dear. Comes of all that coming. She always does a lot after a beating. But I still think that bitch didn't have to cane her as well."

Victoria was thinking. She wanted to get everything possible out of this. After their "light" dinner—caviar and roast grouse, with a '49 Latour to wash both down—the two had slept the sleep of the damned. They had woken up refreshed and rested. And Mémé Pizziani had come in.

He had been all smiling apologies. Evidently his wiring was going right, or something, since he was now convinced of the girls' innocence, that they were—as he put it—no more than "enthusiastic amateurs." He tuttingly regretted the whole unfortunate evening. The three witches had of course been sent back to Nice, where they belonged, on the streets. If they weren't careful, moreover, they'd end up with warm seats themselves before nightfall. Mémé begged to be forgiven. Look—he had sent to their room (er, his room), fetched all their clothes and goodies, and here they were, in the adjoining dressing room. Please to take a look. The house was theirs. The fun of it, that was. Would they not join him for breakfast on the terrace—after a dip, if they liked—at which time he would compensate them for any inconvenience they might have suffered, and also propose a little journey?

Victoria raised an arm and yawned. Thereby revealing one exquisitely mossy oyster. Shaven armpits were absolutely out at Bothington. At least until one of the mistresses insisted. Down on the jetty below a crate had broken open and two of the swarthy workmen were scratching their heads over it.

"Doing a little gun-running. Mémé old boy?" said Victoria.

The dwarf smiled. "Let's call them steel assemblages, my dear. And talking of girl-running, I mean gun-running, just puts me in mind of a small proposal I had in mind for you two."

"A proposal, or a proposition?"

"Whichever. But in view of your ultra-British appearance, and age, and the like, you might be able to do me a good turn. Naturally I'd make it worth your while. And arrange all documents. Have you ever been to Algiers, that beautiful city?"

Victoria said, "So it was a proposition. Peculiar travel suggestions are dancing lessons from God. They teach us the thoughts of Chairman Mao at school, too."

"Play up School," said Joy, hitching up her mini in order to get more golden glaze on her thighs.

"That's what I'm worried about," said the dwarf, breathing ever more deeply—really, experienced as he was, the presence of all this peach-flesh was impressively proximate. "Ibrahim may be supporting the Chinese now. That I'd like you to sound out en route. Any information would be gratefully received, and paid for, highly."

"What's highly?"

The dwarf shrugged. "Same again."

This time Victoria breathed in deeply. "Who's Ibrahim?"

The dwarf smiled, stretching richly. "Funny thing is, I've never seen him. No one has ever seen him on the Côte. Yet they say he comes and goes."

"Mostly comes, I'll bet," said Victoria tartly.

"No doubt. He is said to have a most impressive impalement device. We collaborated over this Middle Eastern thing. In short, Miss Digby, I'm asking you to take him some *schnouf*."

"What's *schnouf*?"

The dwarf's dark eyes twinkled merrily. "*Schnouf*? Oh it's a kind of patented flour, self-raising, I'm hoping to put into production. We want to avoid Customs. It's a white grainy stuff and they always get confused. You could carry it . . . on your persons."

"How?"

"Say . . . in your girdles."

"I hate girdles," yawned Joy.

"Well then, your bra. There and back in a couple of days. We'd make all the travel arrangements for you this end. It might prove quite an experience."

After a moment Victoria said, "What do you think, Joy?"

"I leave it to you, Vikki."

"At the moment I'm vaguely trying to relocate my lost body. But look here, Mémé, it's not such a bad idea. I don't see anything *wrong* in it, I mean. How about letting us spend another day in this blissy paradise of yours here and let you know in the morning. At the moment I feel rather like . . ."

She had been eyeing their host's central body. Relaxing almost prone on the long canvas chair Mémé Pizziani's shirt fell away from his strong brown body, and his thumbs hooked in the black satin of his swim trunks, really no more than a jockstrap to retain his beasthood. Suddenly he released this with a flip, rebounding at both gasping girls and swinging vertical from the hirsute nest of his balls, glaring at them with its good eye demandingly.

"Good God," gulped Victoria.

"Great Scott," said Joy, sitting erect.

It was certainly what the prick was. It was beautiful—long, thick, yet tender-looking with a magnificent mauve corona ringing its solid cobra-head. For a normal man it was immense. For a dwarf it was prodigious.

"Now I know why you get the girls," said Joy, bending to inspect it.

"I was just about to say," said Victoria quickly, standing up beside his chair, "there's nothing I like more after a morning dip than a fuck. If you'd allow me to melt that down for you, sir, I think we'd both . . ."

"I was really wondering," said the dwarf, "whether your friend . . . if she's virgin I could even use an armpit."

"You could use my cunt," said Victoria swiftly.

"She's not virgin," said Joy decisively, also standing up and slithering off her slithery panties.

"She doesn't know how to ride astride," objected an increasingly irritated Victoria. "You'll get a much deeper dip with me, and far smoother ride." And she stepped quickly out of her bikini briefs. "No one can see us up here and . . ."

"Nonsense," said Joy, and she hoisted her skirt to fold into her braided beltlet. "I'm much tighter all through. Everyone says so."

"I'm much more experienced."

"You'll go far longer with me."

"I need a fuck," said Victoria defiantly.

"So do I," said Joy equally so.

For a second the two girls confronted each other, bush bare and arms akimbo, across the increasingly vigorous pillar of unsated desire between them. Mémé Pizziani chuckled.

"I think I'll take the blonde," he said.

"Her snatch is black."

"There," said Joy, swinging over a leg and lowering her crotch slowly towards the monstrous member. "You're always doing me out of things, Vic."

"You wait till we get back to our room, my sweet. Anyway," she concluded in a dissatisfied tone, "I hope it splits you. Go on, get right down on it now."

"Ouuh!"

The dwarf coned up the inflated mushroom of his cockhead and Joy went down on it a little.

"The first two inches don't count," said angry Victoria watching this diffidence with contempt. "Plug her to the hilt, the silly twitch."

He began to fuck upwards with quick hip-thrusts, surprisingly agile, using his beach chair for rebound, like some trampoline, and Joy stiffened, ooohing. Finally she said, "I ther-think I'm going to jer-ker-come."

"You greedy bitch," said Victoria and, seizing the girl's hands behind her back, she jammed her down fully on the slick rod in her belly.

"Eeeeee!" eeeked Joy, trying to lever herself up off it. "Uuuuuuu-eeeeih!"

"Now," said Victoria, fiercely, holding her friend's hands locked behind her back and gripping her nape with the other, "let's see how you like being fucked to the ears, bitch."

The dwarf laughed. He pumped up and down remorselessly and ceaselessly and soon Joy was moaning protestingly, "Ber-but I'm coming . . . *again*!"

She came six times. Victoria shoved the haft of a bone knife up her rectum the last twice. At last, head hanging, spittle hanging from her lips, Joy panted, astride.

"Now let me have it," said Victoria sternly. "She's had enough and more."

But suddenly a rectus of fury overtook the dwarf's dark face. He spasmed like an epileptic, grabbing the girl and doubling her like a suddenly sprung trap. She cried out hoarsely. They rolled heavily off the chair in a wet-locked mass, grunting, while the dwarf shot into her in furious jerks, finally losing her and sending his copious cream over her bewildered face and dress.

"Good God," said Victoria again. The sight of that magnificently clefted ass, streaked with violet weals, rooted to the tree of the man's prick had been almost too much for her. She had to have some relief, and fast. She picked Joy up by an earlobe. A fragile pink earlobe.

"I think you can count on us for that *schnouf* stuff, Mister Pizziani," she said. "Let's call it a round five thousand. Pounds. Or fifteen thousand bucks. What's the difference among friends? Throw in a dildo for free, we could use one at Bothington."

The dwarf said nothing, panting on all fours.

"Come on, you," she said, tugging Joy forward by her moist bush. "There's a cane in our closet, dearie."

"Why? What have I done?" objected Joy, trailing after, one hand holding her panties as if pleadingly.

"Been greedy again, as per, luv. Anyway, you're so ultra-adorably caneable at the moment. No. Don't lower your skirt. No one's about."

As they entered their sumptuous room and Victoria closed the door with a snick, the younger girl turned mournfully—"You're always caning and s-s-spanking me, Vic. It isn't fair."

"Algiers tomorrow, pet."

"How do you want me this time?"

"Touching your toes, just touching your toes and looking penitent, please."

# 7

IF THE SOUTH COAST OF FRANCE WAS SUNNY, ALgiers was a cauldron. Even in her Arnel triacetate nothing, a supersexy fabric of grape (in shade) and the whole thing no more than a swim-suit really, Victoria felt hot and heavy and tight at the airport. The four small cellophane packets secreted flatly in her garterless girdle, which tautly tethered cocoa-colored "Great Length" stockings, felt sweaty and icky. She had repeatedly found herself fidgeting with the loops in the stocking tops that slipped into the girdle's garter tabs during the flight. An Arab in a caftan, his face veiled but for the eyes, had seemed to appreciate the wriggling. His eyes had seemed vaguely familiar, but Victoria thought nothing of it. Or them. Joy, in her short, sweet Gay Gibson of diabolically dark nylon Banlon, had been equally uncomfortable up front. She carried two packets in her D-cups and dabbed at her divide with tissues constantly. The Arab had offered her a sweetmeat. She had—naturally—refused.

At the airport the two girls had been met, as prearranged, by a Cadillac. Driven by another curtained

Arab, the pair had stepped peerlessly into its confines, only revealing the maximum of their teeny-bopper succulence in doing so.

"His Excellency is expecting you."

"Who's His Excellency?" Joy asked her friend.

Victoria shrugged. "How do I know? Ibrahim, I guess."

Ibrahim Mohamed was their contact. There seemed nothing to it. They were simply to hand over their *schnouf* to the Arab, snoop out what they could, and then they were free. Their luggage was minimal—two small airline grips containing spare pantyhose and bikinis and supplies of the pill—they were free as the breeze till their plane back on the morrow. The Caddy began to wind up the tree-lined roads behind Algiers to the suburb of El Biar. The two girls drank in sights and sounds, and smells.

The car was checked by an armed guard at a gate. Victoria whistled. They slid into a driveway past long green lawns being watered by barefoot Arabs. The car pulled up at a vast office block of modern design, shaded by palm trees and presided over by a running sign in Arabic under which ran the legend ORIENTAL INDUSTRIES. Its neon was even on, in the sunlight. The girls were rapidly escorted to a soundless elevator, along blotting-paper passageways and into an anteroom of typing secretaries. They might have been in London. But for the weather.

"His Excellency will see you momentarily," said a stunning young Arabess (for if there were Jewesses, reflected Victoria, then an Arab could also inflect to the feminine). The girl had creamy coffee skin, a white blouse and a bread-and-butter typist's skirt longer than their own. But then, it would have been hard to find one any shorter, and still called a skirt. They sat and sighed.

The office they were eventually ushered into was lavishly low-ceilinged, a teaky place of level surfaces, pots in plants, taped Eastern muzak and much chrome. Seated behind the desk was an Arab in ornate djellaba, but bare-headed. He got up at once and, grinning, held out his hand.

Victoria paused before she took it.

"Josito," she said, a little uneasily, "the Argentinian."

"Alias Josito," said the Arab affably, waving them to chairs. "My real name is Ibrahim. I hope you'll get to know me well enough to want to call me Ibby."

"I fear," said Victoria trying to keep her voice polite yet distant, "you already know me . . . only too well."

The Arab increased his grin. "Inside and out, shall we say. It was extremely agreeable." He turned to Joy. "I never did get to whip you with that converted coathanger, did I?"

"No," said Joy faintly, and also as distantly as possible in the circumstances.

"Pity. I enjoy watching young girls squeal and squirm. You might say it is my passion. I am not a sadist, however. That word was invented by a dying capitalist madhouse, an excuse for all the violence of its death-throes. Here in the new Algeria we have abolished all those horrors." He toyed with a jade ashtray—Chinese, Victoria obediently observed. A picture on the desk showed a signed oriental visage. "Sadism was a social convulsion. Just too bad for the victim." He looked down a moment, then said, "Now then. If you two would kindly hand over . . ."

"The *schnouf*?" completed Victoria. Ibrahim nodded gravely. The girl paused, but there seemed no two ways about it, so assuming a nonchalant air she stood up, turned her back and as decorously as possible divested herself of the cellophane packets distributed about her lower person. After a second Joy followed suit. The man looked at them on his desk, pressed a buzzer and said to the lovely Arabess who re-entered—"Take these to the labo, Ladija." Then they were alone again. He smiled and put his hands behind his head. "One has to be so careful these days. We at Oriental Industries leave no stone unturned. Now tell me—who exactly is Monsieur Pizziani working for on the Coast?"

There was a long silence. Both girls swallowed in unison. Victoria whispered, "Here we go again." Aloud she said, "I don't quite understand what you mean, sir."

"Miss Digby, we don't waste time in the new Algeria. If you tell me I shall pay you highly—and I believe you know my monetary standards are generous; if you don't tell me I shall have to spank you for a naughty girl. It will hurt quite a bit. Which?"

"But we don't *know*."

"You must know. I shall find out." His strong brown hand thumped the desktop. "Mémé's *sgío*, or *caïd*. I want to know who pays him from Marseilles. You tell me and I shall reward you richly. You will be escorted back to England where no one will hurt you."

Victoria ridiculously remembered Miss Nicholson. Her throat was feeling extremely dry.

"Might I have a Coke?" she inquired. It was the wrong question. The Arab nodded, went to the drinks table and procured her one.

"That's better," he said. "Now, what's your price?"

Ramon—Victoria was hectically, desperately remembering. I'll say Ramon. But Ramon who?

"Ramon," she said.

Ibrahim Mohamed tscked dangerously. "Stop playing games, young girl. I am Ramon."

"We don't know," said Joy. "We only spent a day or so with him."

"You were working out of his rooms on the Rue France."

"But I swear to you . . . we—don't—know!" Victoria beat her brow. Fortunately the room had air-conditioning. All the same she was perspiring freely. She should have shaved her armpits for this trip.

"Possibly some ocular demonstration might convince you."

With a grin Ibrahim Mohamed pressed the buzzer.

"Yes, Excellency?"

"Ask Mrs. Willoughby to step in and see me." Then he turned to the girls. "In the new Algeria we don't have slaves." He spoke the word with distaste. "You mustn't think we're all that backward. Slaves are a feature of the final phase of lackey capitalism, which we eradicated, bloodily, some years back. All the same, I am sure you will both soon agree that at Oriental Industries complete obedience to orders is required and exacted, and that it would be best to cooperate with me immediately."

Victoria was about to repeat that they knew nothing, but it was getting somewhat monotonous doing so now and at that moment there came a knock at the door, and in answer to an Arabic word a tall, auburn-haired woman entered in a nubbly little acrylic tweed two-piece of great elegance. She was carrying pencil and pad, wore horn-rimmed spectacles, and looked the perfect picture of prim secretary, all expressionless efficiency. She was a handsome broadfaced woman of perhaps forty.

"No, I didn't want you for dictation, Mrs. Willoughby," and Ibrahim when she had closed the door behind her. "It's just that I happened to have two inadvertent visitors." He hesitated—"The Honorable Victoria Digby and Miss Joy ffrench-Fox-Todde. From England."

The woman nodded politely at the introduction. Victoria half-expected her to say: Didn't we meet at Epsom, or was it the Derby?

"They are curious about our ways." He hesitated again, more lengthily, "I want you to tell them what happened to you this morning."

The woman thought. "I arrived late for work, sir."

"And?"

She appeared puzzled. "I was flogged for it, of course."

There was a silence in the room. Ibrahim Mohamed smiled.

"Our visitors seem a trifle incredulous, Mrs. Willoughby. You will have to pardon their ignorance of our customs. Perhaps you would . . . expatiate."

"Oh yes, of course, sir." The woman seemed to understand. She smiled at the two girls. "I arrived seven minutes late for work and so got seven strokes with the cane."

"Where?" asked Ibrahim.

"In the punishment room, as usual, sir."

"No, I mean, where on your person?"

Mrs. Willoughby frowned. She was clearly finding this unnecessary catechism tedious. "On the buttocks, sir, of course. On the naked buttocks. Bent over the frame very tight. Ali likes us tight for the cane."

"Ali is my office eunuch," Ibrahim explained kindly. "He really hits very hard."

"He certainly does," agreed Mrs. Willoughby. "He broke my skin at five. And after it was over I was hopping like someone on one of those pogo sticks." She smiled ruefully at the reminiscence and addressed the girls like two non-understanding children. Which at that moment they were. "What's more, as it's my second late this month—the buses on the Rue Michelet are hopeless these days, I shall really have to buy a bicycle—I can look forward to a juicy going-over with the martinet before I leave tonight."

"Allah!" exclaimed the Algerian. "I'd forgotten. Haven't checked the late book, er lately. How many do you get, Mrs. Willoughby?"

"A dozen," came the answer with a grimace. "And if I know Ali he'll put them all across the rump. I'll be standing through that directors' party this evening, sir."

Ibrahim joined in her mirth. "You find it effective, however."

"Oh terrifically, sir. I simply hate the cane."

"But, no hard feelings?"

"Except where they hurt most. No," she looked in explanatory fashion at the girls, "I'm grateful for the punishment. My husband died some years ago, and this job keeps me up to scratch."

"Mrs. Willoughby, I see that our guests are still the real Christian unbelievers of tradition. Would you awfully mind . . ."

The woman caught his drift at once. "Not at all, sir." She took off her light tweed skirt, stepping out of it gracefully and placing it over a chair. All she had on underneath was a pair of smoky nylons, tautly tethered to a scarlet garder belt. She turned her back. Across her full, rather loose cheeks were several hot-looking weals, dark, short, blotchy on the right.

"As you see, sir, he used the steel tip."

"Mrs. Willoughby, would you mind very much fetching the instrument, to show it to our guests. It really is a beauty."

"Certainly, sir."

Impassive as a Manet she turned for the door, her tawny bush curling; she went through it without pausing for her skirt, half-naked. Not one of the typewriters in the outer room paused as she passed through. At the

*81*

plus-sign of her buttocks in back Victoria thought she had seen something gleaming. She was growing extremely pensive.

"I assure you, sir. We don't know who this Pizziani character is working for. And care less."

"Did he fuck you?"

"No," said Victoria stonily, getting off a glare at Joy.

"Tell you of my new impalement device?"

"He . . . mentioned it," said Victoria stonily, only less so.

"With that you really feel bunged up, I assure you. Oh well," went on Ibrahim cheerily, "Mrs. W. is a real wonder, isn't she. Our martinets or flails are made of dried sheep's gut. Five thongs each. Mrs. Willoughby will return home this evening with some rather painful sensations at her seat. She won't want to be late again. But here is she, the good woman."

The secretary entered holding out a long bamboo cane, whose last inch was encased in steel. The two girls looked at it very respectfully indeed. Both now saw that the woman, in the one piece of her two-piece, was wearing a wide leather belt to which was buckled a thin strap running down her belly, through her cunt and up her cleft behind.

"I see he put a saddle strap on you, too."

She frowned again. "Yes, that was for excessive movement. I'm afraid I can't take seven from Ali as I used to."

"Show it to these ladies."

"Of course, sir."

She turned, leant forward and parted her cheeks. These were painfully divided by the strap.

"I'm jolly lucky it's not a notched one," she said.

"Explain its purpose," said Ibrahim.

"Well," she said reflectively, straightening, "as the

day goes on it cuts in pretty badly, 'specially at the cunt. It hurts sitting on it, and bending over gets quite a problem. I hate to file in the saddle."

"Yes, the groove thong can be quite deterrent when tight."

"Mine," said Mrs. Willoughby emphatically, "is extremely tight."

"Would you touch your toes?"

"Yes, sir." She did so tentatively, on a sigh.

"You see," he observed, "how well the saddle parts the arse. And discourages clenching during correction. But have you any questions to ask her?"

After a moment Joy said, "Wer-what about . . . I mean, like natural needs?"

Still bent over, exposing to them her well-wealed bottom, the woman said, "I'm afraid I have to forgo those, until Ali sends for me."

"And of course there's always a bung. Now stand up, if you would, and describe your sensations and the procedure of your punishment to these fair ladies, in detail. The one to come this evening."

Mrs. Willoughby straightened stiffly, with a wry grimace. Her face was flushed, but unconcerned.

"How do you mean exactly, sir?"

"In detail," said Ibrahim Mohamed, taking up the lissom stick and bending it. "A lively account of what will happen to you."

"Well, of course," began the secretary promptly, her eyes flicking nervously to the cane every now and then, "I continue to work until six, as is usual here. Naturally enough, during the last hour or so I shall become more and more apprehensive and will have to concentrate especially hard on my work, otherwise I shall only make mistakes—and that will mean I'll be in hot water from you tomorrow, Excellency." She attempted a flat laugh at this. The two girls watching didn't share it. "The last half hour or so is highly unpleasant. The waiting becomes really awful. Then everyone leaves except those due for any correction, which tonight will be me and a girl who was away from her desk too long. She's getting the cane. She'll be sent for first, then when she's had hers she sends me, looking rather the worse for wear. By that time I'm longing to get it over with. I go in to the punishment room and Ali will ask me to strip. He always acts with great respect and, of course, perfect taste towards the staff. When I've done so he will remove the saddle and ask if I wish to be excused. I will probably want to relieve myself, and then he will whip me. For the martinet," she frowned, "it's usually lying on some wide bench or board, with the legs parted and the hands secured behind the back. Some girls would rather get it on the behind then on the back, but Ali knows me by now and I fear he'll place them all across my only too commodious b.t.m.—which, by the way, he massages first with a sort of glycerine solution."

"We don't want to be cruel," sighed Ibrahim, watching the reactions of the girls to this story with interest. "It stops it cutting the skin. And also makes it hurt more."

"The thongs make a meaty whack," continued the woman impassively, "and seem to burrow into one's flesh as if they were alive." She shook her shoulders eloquently—"Brrrh! After three or four you've had enough, with the martinet, I assure you. But I have to go the distance. Peak pain for about four minutes. I was a damn fool to come in late. Is there anything else you wish me to tell, Excellency?"

"Nothing. Just remind Ali that I'd like to watch you whipped this evening. Your tale has quite revived my jaded appetites, Mrs. W. Well done. And when you go, would you tell Ladija to come in, please."

"Certainly, sir." Resuming her pebbly tweed skirt and smoothing it into position the woman murmured gently, "I know one pair of sitters not a million miles from here that are going to be feeling sorry for themselves by evening."

"Woodshed time comes as woodshed time must," said the Arab waggishly.

"So pleased to have met you," said Mrs. Willoughby to the girls, and departed.

Slinky-limbed, coffee-cream Ladija entered almost at once.

"Take a letter," snapped Ibrahim, then added something in Arabic. Without pausing the girl reached under her no-nonsense office skirt and took off her panties. Victoria and Joy goggled. This was becoming a habit. Then the girl went to the desk, cleared it of one or two objects, including the jade ashtray, and hoisted herself onto its edge, first hoisting her skirt under her seat and up. She lay back flat on the desktop with her heels under her macilent buttery buttocks, holding pencil and pad towards the ceiling, ready for dictation. She had on a minuscule garter belt, high nylons and wore her black bush well-cropped: almost a crewcut, Victoria reflected. The well-seamed quim, with its fatty, rather hairless lips, was set right on the edge of the desk. Ready.

Ibrahim Mohamed palped it with apologetic smile. "I always dictate better screwing."

So saying, he zipped down his dejellaba, revealing the rock-like prick Victoria had already felt in her guts. Both girls blanched at its crude musculature. "These I get from Hamburg," he said, reaching into a draw, extracting a condom and fitting it over his penis—the sheath was ruby red and had serrations of rubber around it. "It wouldn't be right to let Ladija enjoy it, would it. There are no whores in the new Algeria."

As he shoved into her, indeed, the girl could be seen biting the back of one hand not to cry out. Then she had her pad in place again. The Arab started to fuck.

"Take a letter," he gasped. "Oriental Industries . . . Monsieur Pizziani, M., Villa Merenda, Cap d'Antibes . . . A.M. . . . no that's the Department, idiot . . . Dear Mémé: The last shipment of small arms you sent me . . . get wider, can't you, Ladija . . . was almost totally defective. Period. No springs for the safety catches, not that those were needed, but all the screws were left-hand instead of right . . . you forget that in the new Algeria . . . Christ! Where was I? So that in their last illegal onslaught the Jewish dung were able to . . . per-per-penetrate . . . *deeply* . . ."

The telephone rang. Ibrahim picked it up. The girl groaned and shifted.

"What!" His dark face darkened. He listened in increasing anger, then slammed down the receiver. He withdrew from his lodgment with a plop. Eyes slits, he gazed balefully at the two British girls—"My laboratories. They've just checked out that *schnouf*. It's common-or-garden flour. Baking powder."

"But of course it is," said Victoria conciliatorily, "that's what *schnouf* is, isn't it?"

"So you knew all the time," he snarled. "Come along, I've had enough of you two innocents."

He zipped his robe. "You too, Ladija. It didn't hurt you all that much." The girl had lain forward, groaning, over the desk with her reaming. Ibrahim gave her a whistling crack with the cane that jerked her straight like a spring. "Not content with sending me . . . dud steel assemblages . . . he now has the gall to think he can pass off flour on me instead of shit."

"Shit?" said Joy.

"Horse," roared Ibrahim. "This way, you two. I mean to get to the bottom of Mister Mémé Pizziani.

Or rather, the top. A little visit to Ali is indicated, I believe."

The room to which they were conducted at almost a run by the increasingly furious Algerian was off the same immaculate glass-and-steel corridors as the rest of the offices. Its interior was dismal, however. As bad as Pizziani's little playroom, only worse. An aching expanse of stone flooring, and chains, and tables and, yes, a trestle, and finally one enormous, bald, grinning Buddha about eight feet tall at one end, advancing with a whip coiled over one shoulder and naked but for sandals and filmy, ballooning trousers caught in at each ankle.

The eunuch kissed his hand to his master and a torrent of Arabic went on. The two girls clung to each other, as Ladija smoothed her skirt—she had not renewed her panties in the rush—and seated herself coolly behind a portable typewriting desk to one side.

"Now then." Ibrahim Mohamed turned. There was a rictus of fury on his face. He had totally altered from the suave Argentinian of Ste. Maxime. "You first," he said to Victoria who was feeling very frightened indeed. "Tell me the name of every man you have seen with Pizziani."

The typewriter clacked in the corner.

"But I haven't," Victoria hectically began. "We don't *know* him. Don't you see. He isn't," she spoke as if addressing a child, "of our acquaintance." The typewriter followed her words. This was getting very panic-making, indeed.

Ibrahim leered forward. "Listen. I could induce an adder up your anus. You've no idea how quickly that relieves constipation. Or have you? The same effect can be achieved by filling your belly with water till you look ten months pregnant and placing you on this spit here. I could pierce your nipples with needles and give you all sorts of interesting sensations through those big boobs of yours. I could sit you on a grille and make rumpsteak of your Popo. Instead of which I'll start easily with you." He turned and grunted away at his henchman. The typewriter chattered merrily.

Joy darted desperately forward. "Please, sir, please. She doesn't know anything. We neither of us do. I swear it, honestly, truly, honest injun."

Ibrahim spat at her. "I'll deal with you shortly, Christian filth. Ali will make that broad backside of yours want to reduce itself in no uncertain fashion. That coat-hanger would have been a treat by comparison."

The eunuch's touch on Victoria's shoulder was soft as a lover's, and he was smiling still.

"What are you going to do to me?" She backed swiftly. "Please. Don't beat me."

"Over here, Christian whore."

Gently, tenderly the eunuch escorted her to one end of the pitiless chamber. Victoria was breathing frantically; all she could see was straps, and thongs, and chains, and canes. She made no struggle when the wide leather belt was fastened round her waist, and yielded but a piteous moan as each wrist was cuffed behind it, one over the other. Not the whip, oh please not the whip. But the whip had miraculously vanished from that sleek and oily shoulder.

"Lie down here, dung."

"L-lie down?"

"Here."

He pointed to the stone floor, just in front of some short iron railing affair. Victoria, her teeth ashamedly chattering, lay down, hands behind her, breast a-heaving, on the cold stone floor. They hadn't even told her to take off her clothes. And the eunuch was kneeling behind her, fixing something.

Suddenly she felt her shoes softly removed and her

legs bent back vertical from the knees. She looked round. What were they doing to her? They were taking her stockings off her, that's what, the eunuch's fingers flexibly and expertly untabbing her tabs for the task. The fear of the unknown was making her stomach cave within.

Her knees were set together and secured at the base of the clever iron railing which held her ankles gripped in their vice behind. Her shins were at right angles to the floor. And suddenly the soles of her feet felt despairingly vulnerable and soft.

"You have a well-padded instep," said Ibrahim, "I am sure you will appreciate our podiatric stimulation of their surfaces. All rosy and excited-looking, just like a good English girl's. Very sexy."

Victoria wiggled her toes. A thong was looped round each big toe and pulled fast to tauten her soles. Both of these were now soldier-straight and aligned together—yes, for the rod. There was no doubt about it now. But what was this? Ali had taken from the wall where Joy cowered miserably, plucking at her mini, a long switch of white or bone-like material. Its last two feet seemed forked or split. It was . . . The Rod.

"Ivory," explained Ibrahim proudly. "It is very rare to find a tusk as long as this and I want you to share with me a connoisseur's appreciation. For this whittled strip or switch of ivory is a real collector's item and cost me a small fortune to acquire. It is inconceivably tough and yet so springy that the split in the tip snaps together on the sole like a veritable pincers. It is perfect for the bastinado."

"Please," Victoria pleaded, "really we don't know anything."

Then the soles of her feet were greased—"We aren't savages, you know, and I don't want to slit the skin"— and Ali the eunuch measured off two paces to the lying girl's left. Silence struck the room like a blade. Victoria turned back her head and sucked in breath.

"Please."

"Twenty, Ali," said Ibrahim gravely.

*Phw-phw* . . . the thin lisping whistle was like some high-pitched bird of omen, or skater's edge perhaps. She awaited, tensing her whole self's self. *Whhh-uick!* The rapier-like ivory sliced; she gasped, straining her torso, then squealed as the true enormity of the pain hit her. Joy's hand fled to her mouth.

"One," said Ibrahim gravely, and added something in Arabic to the eunuch.

Victoria twisted like an eel at the second and suddenly hissed with added pain as she did so. The stone on which she lay had been incrusted with sharp-edged pebbles, flinty stones. She heard her best dress tear. Christ!

"Wriggle all you like," invited Ibrahim politely.

In an access of anger Victoria said, "You think of everything, don't you. *Eeeeee!*"

After about the fifth she couldn't keep from turning and watching the eunuch whipping her feet. At least it only scored her right shoulder and flank that way. The lean greedy tail whickered down from the ceiling and buried cuttingly into the pads of her feet, below the toes. She had never dreamed of such unspeakable pain, always imagining the bastinado less than a beating across the buttocks.

*Whuick, whuick, whuiclllk!* He hewed down regularly and she found herself reduced to a panting, sweating lump of flesh, the red-hot fury in her soles communicating itself to the grinding of her groin against the aching pebbles, the twisting of her torso until a breast popped out, to be scored and scarred on the flints there. By ten she started screaming, breathlessly.

"Stooooop, stop, please . . . I . . . uh . . . oh not

another. Oh oh oh aieeee! Ungh! No . . . I . . . it's not . . . oh oh oh, please, please, *God!*"

When the full twenty had been given, and it was over, and her soles were subsiding to white-hot coals, she lay panting, almost retching, her frock torn, patchy with sweat. Ibrahim came forward appreciatively.

"I like to see a young whore wriggle. Quite warmed your tootsies, it would seem. But no skin broken. Or is there? Amazing. Ladija," he called, "do you have the wherewithal to anoint a heathen whore in the true manner? We discourage prostitution in the new Algeria."

Victoria heard the secretary click-clack forward until she was standing astride her own panting, aching body.

Something made her look up.

"Nooooh," she wailed hopelessly then.

For she had stared up into the matted central groove of the lovely girl, her skirt hoisted to her waist. The vision was of velvety slick surfaces, rounding upwards, the pink slit widening like a wound as Ladija held it open there, and a look of intense concentration crossed her pretty features. And Victoria ducked her face back.

The hot jet hit her nape, then traveled down her spine, soaking her. It was extraordinary how long the girl could go on. Even her skirt was lifted back, the girdle tucked under her buttocks and the cleft well sluiced with the splashy pee—after which Ladija most solicitously put the girdle and skirt back in place. The humiliation was curiously total, and exhausted Victoria burst into tears, sobbing and squirming on the flintheads.

"Now then," she heard high, high overhead, "twenty from the other side. After which a couple across the arse for luck."

Was it three minutes or three centuries later that the Earl of Wrenche's only daughter lay on one side of the stone floor of that dismal chamber, holding her ruined feet in her hands, rocking herself like some wailing matriarch?

"Do you still refuse to tell me, dung?" asked Ibrahim then. "That was just for a starter."

Victoria got her writhen lips to speak. Her wet dress was in shreds in front and her breasts bled in two places.

"I'll invent anything you like," she gasped inaudibly, "but you can't do anything more to me than that."

Ibrahim swore as the typewriter ticked.

"Little girl, I am now going to order you the sewing machine, one of the more excruciating torments devised by our beloved Ali. What you have just felt will be like a Sunday school picnic by comparison. But we shall need your delectable bottom for that. First, Ladija, can you bedung this heathen dung?"

"I'll try, Excellency," said the secretary dubiously, coming forward.

"You. Lie on your back with your mouth open."

Victoria had no strength left to disobey. Again she saw the straddled legs, the parted cheeks, the wink of sphincter ring—as Ladija strained and strained, crouching a little.

"Shit, woman," Ibrahim ordered angrily. But the pretty Algerian had to stand up wryly.

"I just went an hour ago, sir."

"Ali, when you're finished with Mrs. Willoughby this evening give this stubborn sec ten across the top of the legs, will you."

"With pleasure, Excellency."

"With the whip."

"With the *whip*, sir!" The girl turned from her typing table.

"Show me the marks tomorrow, sweetheart."

"Yes, sir."

"See her to the door with a pint of hot olive oil up

her rectum, after. That'll teach her to be costive. She'll break all Olympic records to the groundfloor bathroom, you see if she doesn't."

Ladija sat down thoughtfully. "I might be able to produce one, sir. A small one."

It was too late, evidently. Ibrahim had turned back, increasingly excited (as witnessed the tentpole under his djellaba)—"Now truss this child like a chicken and introduce her to real pain as a treat."

Victoria, bayed, hobbled to the outside edges of her feet. Visions of judo throws filtered through her misty mind. She made a step towards her tormentor, cursed, hopped, grabbed her scalding foot and was quite easily overpowered, cursing and sobbing with frustration.

"For that it'll be three each side."

Even Joy, her porcelain eyes bright with terror, had to admit that her senior school chum made a magisterial spectacle when Ali had finished with her. Suspended in an inverted Y Victoria looked most melodramatic, if scarcely victorious. Stripped naked her melon bosoms, grazed and abraded at their aureoles, stuck rigidly sideways, sweating and tense. Her belly clung to her backbone, while her marked arse clamped over wide-parted thighs. Ali adjusted all the pulleys until she was stretched like a bow-string, then he went over her again, pushing on her thighs for any slackening.

"One final time. Are you going to squeak?"

"You know perfectly well I know nothing," Victoria panted, craning back. "What are you going to do to me now?"

"Along that lowest weal, Ali," instructed the Arab. "Three nice long stitches at the bottom of each chubbie." Ibrahim Mohamed came round in front of her. "This won't kill you, my dear. It will merely make you want to climb around the ceiling a bit and tear off your bottom. It's the next best thing to being bitten on the clit by a scorpion, and twice as good as the blowtorch up your secrets."

"What is it? What's he doing . . . with that . . . *needle*. OW!"

The eunuch had come leisurely forward holding what looked to be a large sewing needle threaded with a length of white wool. Perhaps Algerian sheep? Handling the right cheek with his left hand he inserted the needle into the skin where it was still blood-blue, from the famous cravache, drawing the thread in and out through the integument there. Victoria cried but not loudly. The pain was bad, not impossible. She had always hated the hypodermic, however. She clenched defensively and Ibrahim said, "It will only go in deeper if you do that. Relax and enjoy it."

"What are you doing to me?" Victoria cried, desperate to have the curtain of unknowledge lifted.

"You'll know soon enough."

The thread was left dangling and another stitch was made.

"Give her two minutes between them, Ali. We don't want to be unkind."

When the eunuch had finished she strained back her desperate head. The thread looped at each buttock. He had sewn it into each in three places, each stitch a good inch apart and with the thread drooping down. She was tasseled, behind.

"You are now ready for the sewing machine, my dear," said Ibrahim inspecting his minion's handiwork. "I shall explain the object of the exercise. This thick thread with which your heathen behind has been honored is a sulphurous fuse. It burns slowly, but not too. When Ali ignites it you will have a minute to reflect on your stubborn silence, then—well, have you ever had a hot oil-burn, rather prolonged? No? A bit worse than that, I fear. Thirty seconds or so between each burn, and a nice long interval while it changes sides. The stitches are purely cutaneous, you'd be surprised at how soon the marks will go, though it does tend to leave a bottom like yours . . . a trifle tender.'' He added, ''But after all, it's only fat.''

Victoria had listened with gaping mouth and bulging eyes—in silence. Suddenly as the full meaning of what was about to happen to her dawned on her dazed mind she let out with all her breath—''NAAAOOO-OOOOWWWWW!''

''What an octave,'' said Ibrahim, mock-holding his ears when she had finished. ''I fear we shall have to gag this soprano. Ladija, use her panty-girdle, and a belt. Soil them unspeakably first. Have you any pee left in you, child?''

''Yes, sir,'' said the secretary, rising promptly. ''I do think I might also, sir . . . if you would let me off the . . .''

''Get them good and dirty. Fine. Like that.''

Thus foully gagged, Victoria looked more impressive than ever. A tethered mustang. A caged cougar—the tan line on breasts and back vivid under the spots Ali turned onto her.

''We'll ask her opinion afterwards. This will serve as a good lesson to her to whore. Light up, Ali.''

The match was approached, the fuse hissed, climbing quickly upwards. Victoria, wrenching round her head, snorted snot above her gag. Her eyes widened uncontrollably. The flame was mounting to her flesh.

Suddenly the pulleys creaked as if tugged at by some giant hand. The sturdy body lunged forward in a single scream-stifled spasm—*''NNNNNNNNGHHHH!''*

The fuse was burning through her skin.

Clenched as in ecstasy, her body held its trance, her buttocks jammed rock-hard, till the burn emerged the other side and started its downward trail of the loop before remounting. The girl's body sagged, breathless, sweating.

Joy was on her knees, her hands wringing—"You're *torturing* her. She doesn't know anything!"

"Your turn will come, my beauty. She has five more like that."

*"NNNNNNGHHHOOOOOOAAAGH!"*

The fuse burnt through again. The body spasmed like a puppet's.

After the third the head lolled.

"Quick, Ladija, the smelling salts. We want her awake for these last three."

Victoria suffered two of them, then Ibrahim disgustedly cut the burning fuse—"What a milksop. She's fainted. Let her down, Ali, and give her some brandy, Ladija. I want to see if this other one can squirm as well. She has quite an arse on her, this *pute*. Hallo, what's this?"

For Joy had fled, flinging herself like a madwoman on the door. It was locked. She stood panting, back to it, her body revealed in the clingy crepey stuff, frantic. Then she came windmilling forward at them, sobbing.

Ali easily tripped her. Ibrahim took the ivory switch and flicked it twice across the tender underbum, over which the skirt was flirting.

"Sorry to have to ladder your pantyhose," he said and then, with Joy kneeling, he dealt a thrashing horizontal lash with all his strength and stinging skill. At which he had a sip of pure honey.

The switch clipped in the soft flesh of that peerless rear perfectly. Joy seemed to jump forward a foot on her very knees, grabbing herself with contorted face, jacking straight and twisting on her back for protection for her chubbies.

Ibrahim let his limb rest almost lazily, tauntingly, on

her while she writhed, then flashed it twice, with sickening sounds, across her belly.

Joy hissed and—as he had anticipated—doubled her knees up to her chin, at the same time kneading her injured tummy. Ali smiled at the maneuver, and Ladija felt a flicker of feminine, sympathetic terror flee through her at the spectacle. Between Joy's hinged and lightly threshing thighs pouched out through the transparent hose the slot of herself, the sliced lump of her lymph. The seamed vulva, very rosily veined and poutingly oval, looked tender as a skinned plum. The tip of the switch bit it quickly, like a striking snake, with a snap that seemed to pluck at it livingly.

Joy screamed, stretching. She rolled on the stone floor in a frenzy, holding her hands beneath her.

"Now," said Ibrahim when she had come to rest, "let us take this little pigeon and spank her bottom for her, Ali."

When Victoria came to, the neck of a bottle was a-chatter at her teeth and a burning fluid pouring down her gullet. The bottom of her bottom seemed afire. Ladija assisted her to rest on one side. Ladija was being delightfully attentive.

The far end of the room seemed wholly occupied by bottom. The Bottom. Surely against the tenets of his religion Ibrahim Mohamed was watching the spectacle with a cigar in his hand. Joy had been divested, or had divested herself (Victoria did not know), of absolutely everything. She was very solidly secured by straps to a solid upright stake, reaching to her positively historic breasts. Her hands were held in some way before her. To one side Ali was seated peacefully on a stool, making preparations.

"Getting the terrain ready," whispered Ladija, one arm about The Breast. "You'll find this will enormously improve the action of the martinet."

Barred with a beauty, Joy's crupper cringed as she looked back. Ali had approached his stool. He sat down directly behind her, holding in his right hand a long needle socketed in a wooden handle and placing a lighted blow-torch at his feet.

"She's exciting, isn't she?" whispered Ladija urgently.

"Enormously." Victoria looked at her closely; the brandy had helped a lot. "You too?" she said.

"You forget I'm going to be whipped later."

"I like to watch it," said Victoria primly. "Joy likes to get it. Only pretends she doesn't."

"She's going to get it," said Ladija in her undertone. Her slim fingers strayed. Victoria caught a hiss. "I think you like to get it a bit too, no?"

"I didn't know I was that ready," Victoria murmured back indignantly.

Ali held the needle in the flame until it was glowing. Fixing his chosen spot with the fingers of his left hand he touched the flesh of the flagellated posterior with the needle's ruddy tip. He held it there a second, then withdrew it.

"Help, Vikki, help!" Joy called back imploringly.

"Has the whore woken up?" asked Ibrahim idly, barely deigning to glance in her direction. He was all too obviously riveted to the sight of Joy's squirming bottom. On this had appeared the dark spot, no bigger than a pin's head, of the needle's unholy burn. Ali began to cover the underside of the dimpling derriere with more of the same.

"Hou . . . aaaah . . . oooh!"

Her limbs contracted, she jerked at her bonds. Ali dotted the whole under-area with the tiny blood pustules or blisters and worked now in between the velvet cheeks.

"Pitiless," said Victoria.

"The only way," came back Ladija, still stroking and feeling. "She'll sense it to the marrow now."

"Brrh! Did I writhe like that?"

"Better. Which is to say, worse."

"God, you absolutely soaked me, didn't you. Thanks for not doing the other thing, though."

"Yes, but that whip is hell. However, I'm awfully afraid you two are going to be sent to the camp unless you speak up and say something. By comparison with that the whip is heaven."

"Now give her a dozen, Ali," Ibrahim was instructing. "Only let her hands go free. I like to see them grabbing back like schoolkids."

It was done. Joy turned timorously round, gripping her hands before her. The barbarous martinet with the five gut thongs enlaced around its shiny handle was produced, shaken out. It lay heavy, hanging, five speaking serpents in the air. Then the young figure convulsed. Her head went back, her eyes went wide, no breath came from her breathless mouth as the fangs seemed to hug her livingly. The buttocks made a brusque motion, as if trying to shake them off—five somber streaks appeared and Joy gave vent to the exhalation of a long and hopeless groan.

"One," said Ibrahim.

The thongs drew back, the figure crisped, its hands wringing like mating doves in front of her.

*THWACLK!*

Joy seized her whip-striped cheeks with an anguished cry.

Immediately the eunuch cracked his whistling lash across the backs of her hands and adroitly skinned her knuckles. Joy gave an even more anguished cry and tried to stick them in her mouth. One hand was bleeding badly. Ibrahim laughed cordially.

"Tell us what you know, Christian filth, and soon," he counseled.

"AAAAAH!"

THWLACKKKK!

"Nooooo . . . *anything!*"

Suddenly the Arab said something to his servitor in his most guttural Algerian, and strode forward. Joy was hidden from the hiding watchers by the sweeping folds of the back of his djellaba. This had been lifted up in front, it seemed. There was a pause, a wail from Joy's deepest larynx, the man shoved, gritting his teeth, she rose a-tiptoe, moaning and crying—"Nooooh . . . not there . . . please not there . . . oh uh ooooh!"

Ibrahim commenced a steady pitiless pistoning.

"Silly twit," said Victoria to her now-found friend in sin. "She hates being buggered. Which is to say, she loves it."

"I can't say I enjoy it exactly," came back Ladija, rubbing and stubbing. "Not with his prick."

"It is a monster, isn't it?"

"So you've felt it already?"

"Umm-mnn. He does such masses, too."

"She won't want an enema after this dose, that's for sure."

"Christ, Ladija, you're . . . r-r-r-reaching me, *eeee!*"

"You bitch, sit back on me," Ibrahim was grunting, "or I'll have Ali twist your nips with red-hot pincers. Spread, spread, spreeeeeeaaaaaaa . . ."

"He can't get it any further up her, can he?"

For suddenly Ibrahim had stamped, bellowing as if in fury, veritably well-nigh neighing. Joy, wailing, grasping behind her frantically to push off her impalement, seemed trying to crawl up the post. Ladija and Victoria watched the spasm with amazement. It seemed to shake the very room.

"It'll be limp in a minute," said Ladija.

"And slink pouting out," said Victoria. "What use then?"

Ibrahim had withdrawn, imprecating in Arabic and wiping off his dribbling prick on his djellaba. Growling, he turned to his secretary—"It's no good. They won't talk. Enter these two for the camp. Put some salve on their backsides and ship them out after lunch."

# 8

THE JOURNEY TOOK SIX HOURS. ODDLY ENOUGH, neat Mrs. Willoughby was delegated to drive them, in a battered old ex-British Army truck. She was given her beating first. They heard her screaming. But she sat expressionlessly behind the wheel in her nubbly little two-piece, saying nothing. There was nothing to say, and no one to say it to.

Joy and Victoria sat in the back, under the flapping canvas, extremely well-trussed, gagged and watched over by a grinning one-eyed Arab lout with one gun and three knives which he never ceased honing on a whetstone. The girls had their legs strung together and sat leaning forward, knees up, wrists roped and a stake passing under their knees and over their elbows. It kept them very still. It also kept them very uncomfortable since the boarding of the back of the truck was best Birmingham steel. Joy grimaced behind her soiled gag continually.

On their way through a garage passage behind the massive office block of ORIENTAL ENTERPRISES

Victoria had managed a few polite exchanges with Mrs. Willoughby.

"You're driving us?"

"Not one of those wogs knows his arse from his elbow in a motor car. Just as likely to fill up with antifreeze as essence." She gave a sudden eloquent tug to her tweed, behind. Victoria saw a short red stain there. "I don't know when Ali has hit me as hard as that. He didn't have to skin me on the right." She began packing the driver's seat with cushions.

"Where are we going to?" Victoria ventured in an undertone.

"Beyond Blida. Back of beyond, actually. Transit Encampment Eighteen A."

"Transit? What for?"

But One-eye was coming up, stiff with ropes and knives. The two girls had got in, sighing. The salve had really helped them a lot. Their twin airline bags were inside already. The old truck started up, and they were off, two trussed chickens, bumping and bouncing on the floorboards.

It was dark when they arrived, but the stars were shining brightly. They stretched stiffly when unroped. The air here was cooler. The pair had a sense of a large wired compound, complete with watch-tower, guards, gates. There were a few low huts scattered through this starry somnolence. And the guards were girls. Oriental girls. In trousers, and armed.

"Looks like some sort of Army camp," said Victoria, and Mrs. Willoughby confirmed that such it indeed had been, for the F.L.N. She led them briskly to a long hut painted white. Inside it smelt antiseptic. A girl like a lithe Chinese nurse came forward. She was a lithe Chinese nurse.

"Looks like some sort of hospital," said Joy. And

Mrs. Willoughby, before she took her hand-shaking departure, confirmed that such indeed it was.

"You'll spend the night in here and be thoroughly checked in tomorrow morning. I'm sure you'll be well looked after." She walked off, ruminatively rubbing her behind. Six hours back on that seat did not seem to be appealing to her. What's more, she had missed the directors' party. Where she was quite frequently fucked in public. Surely she was planning not to be late to work any more this month. Or next, for that matter.

The following morning the sun shone brightly on Transit Encampment Eighteen A. The two girls slept long and soundly, like the healthy English teeners that they were. Their rooms were blinded, however, and all they knew of activity outside was a series of short, sharp commands. In feminine voices.

Side by side, in the neat white sterile hospital ward of which they were the sole occupants, they ate the breakfast brought them by Miss Lissom. She could evidently speak no English, and merely sighed and giggled.

"Ham and eggs," said Victoria reverently.

"And ketchup," admired Joy.

"The People's Liberation Army don't do too badly."

Around eleven Lissom returned with a carbon copy of herself beside her and insinuated that our heroines should follow—first having doffed all clothing. Joy accordingly slipped out of the delicious culotte nightie with co-ordinated trim she had on. Victoria slept skinny. They were taken to a surgical chamber, where sat a very surgical-looking Chinese woman of at least seventy summers. Beside this wrinkled crone was a typing secretary. No one present seemed able to speak English.

The girls were given the most extensive—and certainly the most intimate—medical they had ever known. Each detail of this was entered in a large volume stamped in Chinese characters, though on the spine Victoria glimpsed the rubric—ORIENTAL ENTERPRISES—again. Figures were flung back at the sec from the tape measure in the manner of some tailor's establishment.

Ankles, knees, thighs, breasts (even the circumference of each nipple), toes, all were measured and tabulated. The depth of each nostril, the length of each earlobe. Joy's lacerated knuckles, already scabbed, were examined and attended to, as were the small burn marks in Victoria's lower behind. The latter's breasts were the source of some obviously speculative amusement, as was the former's bottom. The measuring procedure ended with a flourish.

Victoria was taken first. She was literally and most ignominiously suspended by her ankles, upside down and then her legs widely parted by the ceiling pulleys.

"Christ, I can't do the splits," she protested as the assistants spread her. The tidy crone approached with her tape. From navel to sphincter, from clitoris to lower labia, Victoria was documented. Finally, a very large simulacrum of an erect male organ in black rubber was inserted in her vagina. It went up and went up.

Victoria gasped.

Lissom-nurse gave a wondering echo.

"That's my womb," Victoria objected. "It won't go in any higher."

But it could and did, and the extent of penetration was accurately recorded. The anal hole was next, both procedures being followed up by specular examinations. An orgasm was induced, and heart and pulse rate taken. Much chattering, here.

Nor was the weighing any less thorough. Victoria was again taken first and the method of assessing the avoirdupois of her glorious breasts was ingenious in the extreme. She was simply strung taut over a steel table like a hammock, horizontal, face down. The pulleys at her wrist and ankle straps stretched her like the rack. Her chest hung pendant, pearlike. A scale came up, with twin troughs for her bosoms, and the weight of each was taken individually, then together. She was then reversed and her buttocks weighed in a similar way. She chuckled when it was over, though her Chinese captors did not. They looked grave over their figures. Over, in fact, The Figure. Victoria's right bubbie had beaten all records.

"Your turn, chum," she said to Joy when it was over. "What's the betting The Bosom beats The Bottom? And I intend all puns."

After the weighing they were photographed. Frankly, they were strobed from every conceivable aspect, and then some. Particular concentration was allocated to the pubic areas. Close up.

"These Oriental cameras are really something, aren't they?" Victoria laughed at one point. She had been ordered to stand straddled over the little beauty, which was remote-controlled and shooting almost all the time. The combined view of twat and butt must have been categoric. But then the camera had been raised on some inner tripod or extension, again by remote control of Madame Crone. Like some insect it rose slowly between Victoria's peerless legs and only stopped when it had snubbed her cunt.

"First time I've been fucked by a camera. What a medical!"

She gurgled with laughter, feeling in better and better a mood. When it was all over they were led back to their ward and each told to put on a collarless khaki shirt with a number stamped in black on the back. Victoria's was about ten sizes too small but Miss Lissom indicated that it was just right. The material was so well-washed as to be threadbare and Victoria's nipples prodded like thumbs at the fabric, her breasts holding the shirt away from her as if it hung from a clothesline.

"Where's the bottom part of the uniform?" she asked suddenly, at a nudge from Joy, equally scantily clad and rolling up her shirt-sleeves. Joy's back had on it a large E-4; her own E-3.

But Lissom was laughing, she had understood, she was making signs. She handed them each a curious lean leather belt, with brass studdings and two buckles. When Joy and Victoria had fastened these around their waists the shirts barely covered the mons in front and hung ridiculously over the shelves of the two sturdy posteriors, in back. They were barefoot. As a matter of fact, when they were left alone, Victoria thought they both looked very zippy and chic in only their shirts.

"Imagine strolling into the Beau Soleil of an evening in these," she said, admiringly.

"Would that we were back there now, darling," Joy replied, giving her a frightened kiss. "How in heaven's name are we ever going to get out of this mess?"

"God knows. Or Aunt Grizel. I don't."

They were not left alone long. A businesslike Chinese woman wearing pale blue slacks and shirt came in with a notebook in one hand. She spoke English and did so with vigor.

"E-3 and E-4? New arrivals? I'll take you over to your hut. Put all your belongings in your bags and carry them with you. Follow me in single file."

Outside they blinked in the sun. The huge rectangular compound was almost empty. Inside its wire surround there were a few Army huts and, near the gate, a plank building with steps up to it of a slightly more impressive nature. It was clearly the main building and a double rank of women, their backs to Victoria and Joy, bare-foot and wearing simply the same lettered shirts, were singing some dismal chorus.

Their escort, hurrying them up a slight hill, looked back—"They're singing their Daily Ode to the Well-Doer. You two capitalist curs happen to have arrived on a holiday. It's Lo Po's birthday."

Who's Lo Po, Victoria wanted to ask, but didn't. She was beginning to feel fairly frightened. She had just seen a small squad of women marching past a hut marked L, their shirttails flipping at their derrières, more than one of which was striated with weals. She looked emphatically at Joy's. Her friend was striding ahead, making hippy little squirms to try to dislodge her shirttail from settling in her peach-cleft. The Bottom was definitely on display.

"That's Liberty Hut," said their guide sharply. "They were all put on Orders and well whipped a day ago. Two of them are up again this evening. That's B Hut over there—Brotherhood. You're E, for Equality. Here you are." She consulted her notebook, ticked off their "names" with a pencil, and pointed—"Capitalist Criminals E-3 and E-4, in there. I'll fetch your Hut Guardian directly."

The girls blinked too as they went in out of the sun, carrying their tote bags. It was a big bare wooden hut with four straight cots in it, a table and nothing else; a door at one end led through to what seemed to be a washing room. There were small lockers beside each bed. And on one bed lay curled a woman, also in a belted shirt. And also exposing most of a beaten bottom. But another was coming softly forward towards them, smiling and extending her hand. She was a stunning tawny beauty of lush proportions, her figure bursting from her shirt and she gave each girl an impetuous kiss.

"I'm Vilma," she said. "We heard two more were being sent over and frankly I'm glad of the company. Welcome to Equality Hut." She spoke in an American accent and drew the two newcomers into the hut, showing them their beds. Victoria chose the one near her cicerone, Vilma. Across the wide aisle, Joy chose a bed beside the other woman, who had not so far moved. "You can put your things in those," said the redhead, gently indicating the lockers. "Please call me Vilma only when we're strictly alone together. We're supposed to drop all names."

She turned an opulent shoulder. "See—I'm really Capitalist Criminal E-1. And in the presence of our beloved Benefactresses we call each other by numbers or," and she eloquently tapped one meaty hip, "mama spank."

"I'm Joy," said Joy. "And this is the Honorable Victoria Digby."

"Pleased to meet you," said Vilma warmly.

"What's with her?" said Victoria, pointing to the occupied bed.

Big Vilma spoke in an undertone. "That's Margot. Alias, E-2. We came here together and have been in for a couple of months. Margot Misery, I call her secretly. And that's why I'm so glad you two kids are coming in. Cheer the old place up a bit. You see," and her creamy forehead wrethed in thought, "Transit Encampment Eighteen A does have rather a lot of awkward rules and regulations. I'll give you the rundown right away. It's . . . rather strict. We do get spanked—as you can see. And Margot takes it awfully hard." She winced at her pun. "Actually, I can't say I blame her; they give poor E-2 a tough time. But come on over and let me introduce you." She gave the cot an amiable kick. "Hey, Margot, wake up and meet Victoria and Joy. They're rooming with us now."

109

The woman sat up, smiled wearily and shook hands with both girls. She was perhaps forty-five with a soft round figure that was only showing the merest sag, yet was mature enough to make the shirt look oddly incongruous. She had her black hair cut short as a boy's—or as some boy's—and this again contrasted curiously with her face, which was well-browed and hyper-anxious in expression. She held her legs close together as they chatted, kept on giving nervous glances towards the door and altogether Victoria decided she beat even Joy out as a picture of the woebegone. Only at school, in the faces of scum about to be beaten, had Victoria seen quite that poetry of pain-to-come.

"Margot's Danish," Vilma explained in conclusion. "Came out here as a translator or something, I rather gather, when they got her. But come and sit on my bed and let me tell you a little more . . . of what you ought to know around these parts. We might as well make the most of it, now we're here."

The extroverted, over-ripe beauty sat at the head of her bed with her knees up and scratched her cunt reflectively. She did not seem to mind showing it at all. Her bush had been lightly clipped or shaved and was bristly in appearance, round a strong pouchy quim. Her clitoris shone, huge.

"Yeah, just what is this dump?" Victoria inquired at once. "Transit Encampment. Transit for what?"

Vilma gave her a long stare from glossy orbs. "Ibrahim send you here?"

"Uh-huh."

"After a little spanking?"

"I'll say."

And Vilma heaved a sigh. "You'd better know it all right away, kids. We're here for sale."

"Ooh."

In the shocked hush Joy said—"White slaves."

Vilma nodded. "Capitalist murderers, of course. Me, I was born in Milwaukee and became—wait for it—an 'Oriental' dancer. Hah! Anyway, an exotic. I was working some real crummy joints in the West when I heard of this offer out here, in an Alger bistro, you know. Of course it was one of Ibrahim's things. They check out girls who have no relatives, friends, travel a lot. My pa and ma died in an auto accident years back. Margot's got almost no ties in Denmark at all, it seems."

"We," said Victoria stiffly, "have all sorts of ties. Almost everywhere."

But Vilma merely shrugged. "Won't help you any, sweetheart. Not in China. Most of our buyers come from China. Anyone see you caught? Any friend, relative? What do you do about getting out of China, kid? Me, I'm hoping I'll be lucky and land a rich Arab. Maybe he'll work me in Cairo, who knows? I'm not fighting it, baby. I like to fuck. But I wouldn't want to be in Margot's shoes. They're selling her for flogging." Her face changed—"Sweetiepie, would you mind not mussing my sheets too much. I don't want to be on Orders tomorrow. We do have to keep this place, applepie."

"What's Orders?" asked Joy.

"Mama spank," said Vilma, rolling her moist eyes.

"I've been spanked," said Victoria.

"Not by Cheeky you haven't been."

"Who's Cheeky?"

"My name for our Block Bitch. I.e., Benefactress. You'll see why when you've met her. She's quite a slinky specimen but don't be deceived—sheer steel under the skin. Sometimes I really think her heart is made of wire and whipcord. But let me give you a runover of the rules and hours."

Victoria saw a pleasant bowl of olives on the table and went to get one. Vilma shook her head.

"Wouldn't if I were you. Aphrodisiac or laxative and sometimes both at once. We get fed like fighting cocks here. Evidently a certain embonpoint is encouraged—must have put on seven pounds since arriving, myself—though in your case I'd hardly think . . . my dear, you do really have the most stupendously firm and solid pair of canteloupes I have ever . . ."

"Thank you," said Victoria gravely.

Then something started happening.

A tawny light flickered deep in Vilma's lovely eyes. Her face paled, went set. Suddenly, as if electrified, both she and Margot jumped off their beds and stood at their heads like puppets, or soldiers on parade, hands at their sides, eyes ahead, at total, unmoving, unblinking and—yes—terrified attention. Fear oozed out of Margot, in particular, like sweat.

For a shadow had fallen in the doorway. A slim and shapely shadow. The girl who came in might have been twenty-two. Soft-cheeked and smiling, her Chinese eyes only slightly slanted under her silky crop of ink-black hair, she brought in terror with her.

Victoria did not know how or why. Perhaps it was in her tigerish gait, that physical containment and total relaxation of the athlete—some sense of menace, at any rate, made both girls move in a subdued way and take up similar positions in front of their own neat beds. The girl watched them, silent, motionless. She had on thonged sandals and her thin blue linen slacks were so skintight a frogman might have found them slightly suffocating. Where they fitted behind, they could have been pasted to the pair of snubly arched cheeks, so curved, and tender—yes, Victoria suddenly knew why Vilma had named her Cheeky. This was a succulent specimen in mint condition, a dishy dollie if ever there was one. Above the waist the pale blue shirt was knotted under the round rims of the high breasts, exposing the bare-fruit waist, with its dimpled navel. The girl could have done honor to the Beau Soleil or even the Ritz. Looking at her, Victoria had her first feeling of feminine inferiority, everything was so marvellously made and articulated, and at the same time she had a curious sense of having been suddenly drained of all energy. At her waist the Chinese girl wore a leather belt; to this was clipped a small bunch of keys, a revolver, and a switch—this on her left side. She spoke quietly and without emphasis, in an unaccented English.

"You are the two whores, I understand. Good. We discourage prostitution in the people's republic. I personally had the pleasure of shooting one of the last pimps of the Casbah. A Corsican, a very rotten man, we brought him out here and set him up as a target. I must have put a dozen bullets in his stomach . . . and his rump, his great fat bum . . ." She held her hand to her mouth like a child restraining laughter. "We made him die so slowly. It was gorgeous. But it's easy to kill a man; making him suffer requires imagination . . . genius."

Victoria was aware, out of the corner of an eye, of Margot literally shivering.

"Here you lose your names," went on the girl amicably. "You are E-3 and E-4. Never let me hear you using your names or you will feel this." She tapped her switch. "Originally we used to give all our imports the names of celebrated murderers, but it got too complicated. Better like this. At Eighteen A you are going to be reduced to a digit, a stock, a stone. Not even a thing. Nothing, understand?" She paused in front of Victoria. "You, E-3. You're the one who got the sewing machine, aren't you?"

"Yes."

"You address me as Benefactress."

"Yes, Benefactress," Victoria found herself saying very quickly.

"Show me. Turn around and bend over the end of the bed. So. Good. Here? Very interesting. All right, you can stand up now. I like whipping girls' bottoms, E-3, and I shall enjoy whipping yours, and E-4's too. The trainer or tail of my switch is wound in wire and stings unspeakably. I shall whip you often and without mercy. It will never be intolerable but always agony. You will grow—not to hate me, because you will soon lose all human feelings—but to *recognize* me from deep within. As an anti-self, a presence of annihilation in your consciousness at all times. Never letting you rest. Supervising your movements constantly. Isn't that right, E-1?"

"Yes, Benefactress," replied Vilma instantly, in a loud tone.

"Tomorrow morning at five o'clock a gong is beaten. If I should find you still in bed when it finishes *you* will be beaten—after I have given you ablutions. If I find a speck of dust in hut inspection I will whip your bottoms mercilessly. An insect on the floor, and you will kneel down and eat it. I shall enjoy making you suffer, knowing that I am doing my duty in the peasant movement of all the people. E-3 will work in the laundry, E-4 in the kitchen." The girl broke off to laugh softly. "E-2," she said pointing to Margot with the tail of her switch, "that corrupt hyena shivering like a jelly over there, why, she works on road stuff, breaking stones and the like, to put a little muscle in that flab. She's old but with a bit more work we can get a good price for her as a victim. What were you whipped for yesterday, E-2?"

"Looking insolent, Benefactress," came the immediate, unsteady answer from Margot.

"How many did I give you?"

"Eight, Benefactress. Thank you very much."

"What with?"

"The rope's end, Benefactress. The Persuader."

"Bring it here and show it to our guests."

At once Margot moved. Her bottoms jouncing she went to the doorway to the washroom. On one side of it there was a hook and hanging from this was a short stretch of hard rope; Margot took it off and holding it in the looped end came forward to the center of the room.

"This is the Persuader. I had it made specially, and the tip dipped in tar to make it really hard. It is kept wet by you. If I find it dry I will whip the whole hut. The water lends weight. Others of us like other instruments. The Benefactress of Liberty, for instance, was actually at a girls' school in England, like you two here, and favors a long thin cane. I used one myself for a while. I liked to see it cut into the soft buttery flesh, and still do. I experimented with many methods. I even once used a flat paddle, as do the Yankee imperialists, and enjoyed the way it made the bottoms of you hyenas bounce. But all in all, I have come to like my Persuader which stings and bruises too. Above all it is pleasant," went on the unaltering formalized little voice, "to see the bite and nip of the switch on skin already tenderized by the rope. For more serious offenses you are put on Orders, and appear before the Well-Doer at six in the evening; your bottom is usually thrashed to ribbons quite soon thereafter. Than Orders, there is only one more severe punishment and that is a public flogging in the square. I would like to see both of you, E-3 and E-4, flogged and will seek every chance I can to try to get it ordered for you. You will almost certainly be up before the Well-Doer now and then, and I assure you the only possible policy for you is to rid your mind of all ideas in my presence, and become as the lowest of the low. After a month you will be supple as gloves, mentally speaking. You will be as unthinking as plants, able to contemplate the utmost degradation without so much as a ripple of reaction. Let me give you an example. Stand out, E-1."

Vilma came quickly forward, her head high, and stood looking straight ahead in the center of the aisle.

"If it won't confuse you too much to answer, who are you?" she was asked.

"I am class enemy E-1," said Vilma instantly, in a loud clear tone of voice. "I am a gangster of the corrupt capitalist West, a jackal and lackey of imperialism. I beg to have my crimes pardoned and to be corrected as to what ideas I may be allowed to entertain."

"What is your greatest desire at the moment, E-1?"

"The highest paradise you could accord me at this time, Benefactress, would be to allow me to lick your feet, in atonement and humiliation."

"You may do so, E-1."

The level stare that met Victoria's eyes, as Vilma dropped to her knees and proceeded to lick carefully inside the bony yellow toes exposed by the sandals, sent a thrill of terror running up her marrow. This was indeed sheer steel—cold steel, too.

"Stand up, E-1. Now, have you any further favor to ask of me this day of Lo Po's birthday?"

Flushed and erect, there was a pause in Vilma's voice as she said—"Ner-nothing that I can think of, Benefactress."

The Hut Guardian gently unclipped her switch and held it across her lithe and lovely body.

"Are you quite sure of that, E-1?"

Without obvious effort Vilma spoke—"If you would condescend to correct me, physically, I should of course regard it as the highest of possible honors, Benefactress."

"You wish to be punished?"

"Passionately."

"Where?"

"Across my miserable bottom, Benefactress."

The girl gave a girlish giggle and winked at Victoria—"After a week I know exactly what everyone likes least. Hold out your right hand, E-1."

Vilma did so. The girl walked well to her right and measured aim. "The hand that grabs for money," she said, as if to herself, "filthy with cash . . ." She frowned in concentration, said, "Just a little higher. Good." Then with almost a bowling motion she brought the eel-thin quirt raking across the outstretched palm. The wiry trainer bit. Vilma gasped and her head went back. But she held out her hand as if feeding a horse. She was in profile right in front of Victoria.

Two, three, four, five. The hurt hand fluttered like a dove, its surface scarlet. Vilma hissed with pain. Six, seven, eight, nine . . . it went on and on. After ten, she gripped her right wrist with her left hand, forcing herself to keep her hand out steady. Eleven, twelve.

"Now the other."

Miserably shaking her hand as if it had been bitten by frost, rather than lancinating heat, Vilma squirmed in place. She slowly held out her left. It too received twelve lashing, cuts and when they were over the woman grabbed her armpits, hopping with pain; the nearest side of the shirt to Victoria was marked with blood when she took her hands away.

"Poor E-1," said their Hut Guardian, as if consolingly, "You do hate it so on the hands, don't you! And I believe you did think it was all over, and that you wouldn't have to put them both out together for another dozen."

*117*

"Benefactress," was the puffing protest in reply, "I don't believe . . . I could . . ."

"Don't you remember," said the slender girl mournfully, "how unpleasant it was when you made a fuss before? How you had to go and kneel and have your hands held out in the stocks and they looked more like cooked beef than anything when it was over? And her face"—she turned impishly to Victoria and Joy—"it was just like one of those Christian martyrs."

Tears running down her cheeks, Vilma held out both hands together. Her Benefactress straightened the fingers and stood to one side.

Pfuittt! . . . huitttt!

Three, four, five, six, seven . . . a cry of some trapped hare escaped the bitten lips . . . eight, nine, ten, eleven, twelve. Vilma, tramping the floor, her face searching the aching ceiling as if for relief, still held her hands before her. The quivering, bleeding palms might have been seeking alms.

But no alms were accorded them.

"Have you any further favor you require of me, E-1?"

And Vilma wept.

*"Force yourself!"* was suddenly spat at her, through gritted teeth.

There was a long pause, then Vilma's agonized voice sliced through it on a sob—"If you wish . . . if it would please you, Benefactress, to take the trouble to give me a few more strokes . . ."

"Good. You may go back to your bed." The girl turned in explanatory way to Joy. "The mental effort of saying that is something you two would not yet be up to. But a little training will soon work wonders. No, ordinarily I will whip you on the buttocks. E-1 is an exception. E-3 may respond to applications across the breasts, we'll see. But for normal purposes I use the Persuader across the bare bottom, slightly bent. I like the flesh to be fairly slack." She felt Joy's right cheek with a testing hand. "I suppose it was Ali who made those naughty marks. You I shall always beat on the bottom, and I hope to see you publicly flogged across it, too. Now, when I call for position, it's like this."

Before their mesmerized eyes the girl reclipped her switch and leaned over with her hands on her knees. The perfectly proportioned littly fanny, high, liquid yet lively looking, curved its cubs under the soft skintight stuff. Not a wrinkle, not a crease. You couldn't so much as get a razorblade between skin and stuff, thought Victoria, eyeing the butt appreciatively; she must have put those on with a shoehorn. Correction: with shoehorns. Suddenly she realized it was a pair she would love to beat.

Whether the Chinese girl read her mind she did not then know. But a mischievous light entered her eyes and, still bending over, she looked up, saying, "Come to think of it, let's have another demonstration. Here, E-2."

Margot had been watching the scene more and more miserably, still holding on to the length of rope since she had not been ordered to rehang it. She advanced with crisped features.

"Give me a couple with the Persuader."

There was a shocked hush.

"Just for sound, shall we say."

"Ber-Benefactress . . . !"

"Across the bottom."

Margot looked bleakly about. She held the thong as if infected. A panicky look came into her eyes.

"I . . . you . . ."

"Hurry up, capitalist louse."

Margot moved her feet. Somehow she got herself behind the bent girl. Almost in tears she steadied the rope. There was a long and ghastly silence.

"I, I . . ." Her arm moved. It rose then wavered, then fell to her side. In a flurry of sobs she dropped to her knees, "Please, please . . . I can't . . . Bene . . ."

The girl straightened slowly with a triumphant smile. "You see," she said, looking fixedly at Victoria. Then she took the rope from the trembling hand before her. "Get up, you, and assume the position. Disobeying a command usually means Orders, but I'll make one exception for today. After all, it is Lo Po's birthday."

Margot bent forward, her hands on her knees. Her shirttail hardly had to be raised behind, but was so. Her full bottom was set close and very soft. The wet rope whacked into it four times, visibly lifting the flesh with each blow. It rested, then whacked four more.

"Now go and stand in the doorway," the moaning woman was told. "Bend down and touch your toes with your back to the compound so that everyone passing by can see what the underside of a capitalist hyena looks like."

Victoria knew icy terror. She was staring straight ahead, not daring to look. Vaguely she was conscious of Margot moaningly obeying. But the silence went on. A spider gripped her spine. Her throat drained dry.

For the Chinese girl was standing before her and the silence was flowing like a river. Her breasts were shivering like jellies.

"Do you cane girls at school?" came a far and even voice.

"I . . . I," but her throat felt gripped as in some vise, "usually I see them caned, yes."

"Just now, when I assumed the position, you imagined what it would be like to whip my bum."

"Yer-yes. Benefactress."

"That's having insolent thoughts, capitalist pig of a whore. I asked E-2 to beat me, and she could not. I did not invite you to, and you did. I shall introduce you to your first Orders this evening. You will parade outside the main building at six. The Well-Doer will allot you a certain number of strokes across the naked bottom. It will be very painful. And tomorrow you will clean me, after I excrete. With your tongue.''

## 9

PROMPTLY AT TEN OF SIX (THE RITUAL FIVE MINutes before five minutes before) four girls formed line under the eagle eyes of their Hut Guardians outside the main building of the encampment. It was as wretched a rank, Victoria (number three in line) reflected, as ever waited outside the door of Bothington Gymnasium after Evening Prep.

Wretcheder.

The girl directly in front of Victoria, a short stocky Hungarian blonde with rather a plain face, all things considered, was actually weeping already. The sun was sinking behind the watch-tower over the wire, in which the smiling figures of armed guards (all female) could be seen. Victoria stood to attention, mechanically ready to follow procedure, for the afternoon of Lo Po's birthday had been spent in a summary of protocol by helpful, red-headed Vilma. It was not very complicated. They were slaves. As Joy put it with a discontented *moue*—"Why even bother to sell us?"

"We don't all like it as much as you do, idiot," had been Victoria's snappy retort to that one. "You seem to forget that it's my butt that's in for it tonight, not yours."

"She's always caning me at school," Joy explained with an eye-roll to reclining Vilma.

"Not true," rapped Victoria.

"Well," said Vilma with a sigh, "I fear you two are going to learn in these parts that there's one hell of a lot of difference between political and pedagogical punishment. Try to avoid Orders. Mama spank."

It was just enough. Victoria was shivering in the last, lancing sun. The four girls were quite naked but for one feature. The rather attractive belt they wore over their shirts was drawn tight around each yielding waist and to it was affixed a slender, cutting chain. This ran through the legs in front, being carefully threaded into the cunt, and was drawn excruciatingly tight up the divide behind, where it was securely affixed to the buckle of the belt in back. Victoria barely dared to move. One link of this minute (so Chinese) chain was horribly crimping her clit. Any moment and . . . the Hungarian in front of her gave a fatty shudder, as if to throw flies off her rump. Obviously she was being hurt, too. Her bottoms were so deep, however, the saddle strap (as Vilma told them this constriction was known) was quite lost in the rich ambery depths. Mrs. Willoughby had been kindly treated by comparison.

The four girls were naked, but their hands were held behind them by a simple (surely fiendishly Oriental) device—a thumb-thong, or rather two. Moreover, round each neck had been strung a crude slice of board lettered, in Victoria's case, BOURGEOIS CRIMINAL SENTIMENTS.

Suddenly sharp commands barked out. The four were marched inside. The interior of the main building was one, Victoria thought, that needed nothing more than it had. It was total communication, in the way the

Bothington Gymnasium also strove to be (never in her life again would she see a vaulting horse, would she smell that slight twist of carbolic in the air, without thinking of beatings). The group was herded outside a plain deal door. The first girl was taken in by the silky-locked Hut Guardian in charge of Liberty. MENSTRUATING WITHOUT PERMISSION CRYPTO-MENSHEVIK DEVIATION read her sign. She was a liquid-limbed beauty, probably from the Caucasus.

Victoria stared in front of her.

In front of her was the Hungarian. Smaller than herself this girl was possessed of hard thick flesh, and a rather curious figure. Short blonde hair fell on sloping, nineteenth-century shoulders, and her waist was really minuscule, but her bottom broadened outwards until at the base it was very strong and heavy. The overhang was immense, almost sterterous in appearance, one made for the positive whip.

A sharp Chinese command. The girl went miserably in.

When Victoria's turn came to enter the Orderly Room, where sat the Well-Doer, she remembered everything except that she had to kneel. Suddenly she was hissing like a cobra with pain. Cheeky's switch cut bitterly into her calves. She bounced down, her placard swinging off her magnificent thrusting bosom.

Chinese was exchanged. The Well-Doer was a sort of Oriental Moshe Dayan, eye-patch and all. Finally he leaned forward over his perfunctory, Army-style desk and said in guttural English—"These criminal activities must be ceasing, E-3. As this is your first offense before us . . . fourteen strokes."

Cheeky interrupted: "If I might be so bold, Sire, this is a hardened capitalist criminal whose mind has to be totally eradicated as soon as possible. I humbly request the full sentence for this repulsive crime. Sire."

"Very well." The Well-Doer yawned. "So be it. Eighteen."

"In there!"

Victoria was unceremoniously thrust into a long planked room which spelt, as no other, the word CORRECTION. It was bare but for the necessities, and it was peopled by two orders of beings: (1) the punishers—two tall Chinese girls of great beauty, grinningly taking practice swishes with their agonizingly long switches at one side, and (2) the to-be-punished—two tethered victims looking as if they hoped the floor might swallow them up. Victoria joined the latter. There was a long, low bench directly in front of her.

When the final fourth girl had been sent, crying, out to join them, Victoria felt her inner skin begin to goose and prickle. The taller of the twain with the switches—evidently top girl—came back from the Well-Doer's office with a large card on which, it seemed, their sins were inscribed. And their sentences. Victoria was interested in the technique. She had heard about it from Vilma, and was intrigued. She had never seen a rapid beating.

But there is something Vilma has not told her.

"Come here, you," says the whipper to the first girl.

She is yanked forward by an ear, her placard removed. She has lovely apple-like buttocks, perfect for cutting into with the switch.

The bench (thinks Victoria) is interesting. It is not complicated. Nothing connected with chastisement (yes, yes, *that* is the word) should ever be complicated. It must be heroically simple, exact, and—of course—just. Hieratic.

Mewing with fright already, the girl is laid down. She lies on her belly, her golden side upward. Straps secure her knees and ankles. But the bench is arranged so that from the waist on she hangs down, her torso touching the floor, her arms still held behind her. She falls helplessly to the boards. But her buttocks are bisected by the strap (or, rather, chain). The bench is not high. But still it is hell. Latches of barbed wire are criss-crossed over her milky thighs and calves when she is finally readied.

And this is far from all.

The two grinning guards, in their fitting slacks, arrange the body so that it is no more than that. The feet are secured about six inches apart. The lithe legs run together. The buttocks are simply *there,* presented perfectly—loose and scared, like fluttery doves. Almost unmarked. But not quite.

From the waist on she lies limply forward, on the flooring, her hands behind her, her sweet face on the boards.

The two girls who are going to beat her exchange excited chatter. Victoria knows what is to happen. Vilma has told her. Both guards now cut their cruel switches through the air, in final practise.

"Eighteen strokes," says one, "take a deep breath, baby."

So saying, she smilingly raises the head, indeed the whole torso, of the about-to-be-whipped young girl off the flooring by a grip on the back of the neck-hair. For a second the girl is almost horizontal. There comes a sandaled kick at a floor ring and, lo and behold, a small panel slides back to reveal an immediate reservoir or pool of scummy liquid. The girl holding her victim lets go, and the latter falls with a splash into the muck. Her head disappears. Placed as she is, her arms behind her, she cannot raise up.

Exactly at once the two whippers take their switches and, standing either side of the low bench, they cut brusquely in.

SWHIPPP! SWHIPPP!

They do so in a rapid cadenced rhythm, each stroke falling with desolating velocity—in a second or less of its predecessor. The effect on the punished person is electric. It is, indeed, just as if some voltage had been passed through the recumbent body.

Recumbent?

Not entirely. The torso twists, it jerks and writhes, as the cuts go on the girl tries to lift herself out of her little well of muck, in which tell-tale bubbles appear. Oh God oh God, thinks Victoria, waiting.

BOURGEOIS CRIMINAL SENTIMENTS.

Very good.

Eighteen cuts, and cuts is the word that describes them. The wiry tail winds in with hideous penetration. Blood flecks the writhing mounds already. The chafing chain fairly tortures the squirmy seam thrust (self-protectively) up. The body tries to rise.

When it is over, perhaps only twenty seconds has ensued. It is a curious kind of punishment. But who would deny that it is effective, as the released girl, her head dripping, wriggles on the boarding as if possessed. It is the Hungarian's turn next.

Terrified Victoria feels terror in her guts. This is shortly to happen to her. (My God my God!)

But what is happening to the Hungarian is exciting. She knows this woman was designed for punishment, she has had it in her since her birth. May she get it, then, *now!*

The Hungarian with the broad hard hips is laid on the bench, secured almost deferentially. She is . . . all ass, and the whippers must do this marvel justice.

This superbly shaped deep buttock demands only the best. The best is accorded it. Her head in the sink of slime she is cut . . . if the cliché is *to ribbons*, then so be it. Each cut is a marvellously placed and worrying agony, deep in the sulcal crevice, that sends the hips bounding as if a very strong voltage were being unleashed through them, indeed, and tears the thighs on the restraining wire. The girl writhes on her back when it is over.

And now it is Victoria's turn. She is fastened down, bump up. Eighteen. Nine either side. Twice nine let it be, then.

Her hair holds her up.

A gentle voice says in one ear—"Take a deep breath. And count yourself lucky, E-3. You get a free shampoo this way."

"OW!"

But the slime stifles her screams (is there urine in it, too?). Suddenly Victoria, as the ripping switches ply about her inferior parts, realizes that this is impossible. No one can absorb a beating of this severity without breathing. She tries to get her torso up, up. Fails. Snorts into the filthy water. Swallows it. Sobs. Starts to drown . . . and panic.

The licky cuts continue, slicking into the young puppyish girl-fat. Causing agony.

She later returns to the Equality Hut in a daze.

But all the days are a daze. Each begins with Ablutions, after the gong is beaten. The four inhabitants of Equality stand on a low bench in the washroom and are hosed down with icy water.

"Turn round. Bend over. Your legs apart. I want to clean your capitalist arses."

The jet strikes the anus. Then the jet mauls at the bubbies. The Persuader is brought into play. It is employed quite often, in fact. The wet rope whacks agonizingly. Joy has never felt anything like it before.

Breakfast, as other meals, is taken in a large communal mess-shed. Each capitalist criminal has her hands behind her in thumb-cuffs and must kneel to eat, licking and lapping at the tin plate put before her.

This contains, amongst other things, a good degree of psyllium seeds, thus ensuring a bulky stool on the morrow.

Such excretion takes place in the washroom, over a long canal through it. The girls squat over this and drop their glistening, girlish turds in front of the Benefactress. If they do not, it's a quick syringe of hot oil up the anus. Something to make you really hop.

Joy works in the kitchens, Army-style Nissen huts with blistering temperatures (in fact, one punishment is to work in them in furs), while Victoria is assigned to the laundry, a low tin-roofed place where a rank of silent, frightened capitalist criminals beat out soaking linen over an inclined board. Watched by a smiling supervisor, in this case a vast Negress, an immense Hottentot.

Yet afternoons are for idling. Vilma is in fact being fatted up, a mass of buttery femininity being considered worthy of high prices in Istanbul. Margot slogs away on the roadwork. It is all very, very sad.

They are allowed to walk around, though not to talk to others.

Once Victoria is strolling back to her hut when a fierce flick of pain in one thigh—accompanied by a feathering of air behind her—makes her duck to inspect. A short, yet fairly thick dart, tapered with red feathers, has lodged in her leg there. Christ, how it hurts.

As she bends to examine she hears a chortle of laughter and almost immediately experiences a savage pain in her stiff right bum-cheek. She cries, and plucks. Another dart, wet with her blood, comes out in her grasp. Hectically she stares around.

"Too close to the wire, idiot," comes, a noncommittal hissing. "It's the watch-tower. They love shooting at . . ."

Victoria darts away, yet not before another fiendish dart has thucked into one breast. She tears it out with terror.

Cheeky thrashes them constantly, and with vigor. Something deep in Victoria's inner self acknowledges this expertise. Bending over, watching a knot in the boarding of the floor take sudden, dancing shape, she knows she is being dominated as she has never been before.

She knows she is slipping into another existence, one for which her whole upbringing has prepared her.

# 10

THE LIFE OF THE CAMP CONTINUES. TODAY MARgot works breaking stones with a bung up her anus, held in place by a remorseless saddle strap. A large glycerine suppository or "rectal evacuator" is liquefying in her insides and beginning to cause her signs of crisis. She has been judged guilty of moral turpitude, to whit having bourgeois ideas about privacy. Her shirt is to be made shorter.

Vilma is whipped. She whips well, half bent with hands on knees and tail of shirt tucked up. Cheeky gives her six with the Persuader, and then makes her kneel down. E-4, or Joy, is bidden lie beneath her on her back. She must lie so that her eyes are under the hairy cunt with its moist sliver or spear of flesh at its head. The beating is continued and Joy blinks disobediently. The fat is whacked inches off her nose. She sees the little ripplings and squirmings of the inner flesh. Vilma is bidden go down on her. It is done. The big burlesque dancer nibbles Joy's growing clit and nearly nips it nastily as the next cut falls. Joy's eyes see the red bar thicken at the bottom of the buttock, feels the sense of light growing in her guts. She is going . . . she is ger-going . . . to . . . .

Joy comes in spasms as the whipping continues.

Victoria stands with her eyes dead ahead, her hands held behind her back in thumb cuffs. She is in the center of the hut. The other prisoners look on.

"Is there any reason why I should not whip you, capitalist criminal E-3?"

"No reason at all, Benefactress."

"Is there any reason why I should do so?"

"Many, Benefactress."

"Name one."

"To eradicate my bourgeois ideas, my corrupt thinking."

"Very well. Fetch the Persuader."

Victoria goes to the wall by the door. Gently, most carefully, she lifts the length of rope off its hook by her teeth and brings it in her mouth to the Chinese captor.

"E-1," snaps the latter. "Why am I punishing this hyena?"

Vilma says at once, "For her crime of being hostile to the dictatorship of the proletariat."

"Stand here and bend forward, E-3."

Victoria leans over. Her tiny tail of shirt is raised.

"No. Keep your eyes open."

There is a very long pause.

The hut is full of the silence of impending pain.

Suddenly the wet rope whucks into the young bottom.

There is another wait, another stroke—THUNK!

Victoria's face squeezes with pain. Twice more searing agony lashes her round bottoms. She jerks, gasping.

"What's wrong, E-3?"

She doesn't know what to say.

"Are you in pain?" solicitously inquires the Chinese girl. "Is that it?"

Victoria dumbly hangs her head. Her rebel feet still pace.

"When you acquire the correct ideology you will no longer feel pain, E-3. Bend down and expose your corrupt buttocks properly."

A girl kneels in the Cleansing Chamber. Her hands and neck are held in stocks, her face appearing to crane forward with a most comical expression on it—anxious to the point of absurdity, the mouth wide open, the eyes trying to swivel round. She is naked. It is Joy.

The class in sexual re-education stand to attention, watching her. A guard looks on with ready switch.

Joy's legs are parted and between her thighs stands an instrument resembling a movie projector. From this an oiled plunger thicker than a penis and made of black rubber is pistoning in and out of her anus. Her cheeks contract, she moans and her lips dribble as it slickly oozes forward into her. A roughly lettered sign hangs from her neck by string: CAPITALIST CRIMINAL BEING EDUCATED IN SODOMY. *Ten minutes*.

She has four more. Sweat beads on her forehead.

The guard consults her bright Swiss watch.

"We shall now proceed to full penetration. By this time the bowel sleeve has grown accustomed to the dilation and there is no fear of any rupturing. Subject was given high colonic before this practice. I shall now slow the plunges but add an inch. What is more each insertion will now be completed by a spurt of hot oil in her entrails. I want you all to watch her stomach closely because the griping effected is quite considerable. Indeed, short of childbirth it is said to be unlike anything else."

The guard moves to the switches. A mewling sound,

like a kitten being slowly strangled, emerges from Joy's opening mouth. She ceased screaming two minutes ago.

Margot has been marvellously marked.

She sits in the center of the square in a re-educating body box. This is a solid box enclosing all her body and leaving only the head sticking out of the top. It is, in fact, made out of old packing cases. ORIENTAL ENTERPRISES had to be erased from one side, to permit the letters CORRUPT RINGLEADER OF CAPITALIST LACKEYS to be put on it. All passers-by have to spit at the criminal condemned to the body box. Margot has been there half a day and her cheeks are streaming with spittle.

Or perhaps it is also tears?

Moreover, the diuretic diet has had its effect. Twice.

Margot is sitting in her urine and her face is tensely frowning since she is trying not to shit.

In the steaming laundry room the line of girls lean forward over the sloping shelf on which they pound the garments. They work silently, watched over by the enormous Negress guard.

Every now and then the guard wanders for a little amusement down the line, whacking an ass here and there with her heavy, serrated laundry paddle. She particularly likes to stop behind Victoria's inclined body and slap the sweating, sturdy seat which the wet tail of shirt barely half-covers in this posture. This young English flesh jounces so nicely, and it is getting nicely wealed.

"Work harder, dog of a Wall Street spy."

But an hour later, when the guard is reading her Mao at the far end, Victoria whispers to her neighbor without stopping her work—"I've got to go."

The other, a tall blonde, says nothing.

"I absolutely have to."

A finger touches Victoria's plump right arm. It points.

Victoria looks down the line, straightening slightly. Her friend has pointed to a bent bottom three away. Between the bare feet a tawny turd lies on the stone floor. And even as Victoria watches the lovely legs part and stiffen slightly, the sphincter swells and widens and another remarkably heavy sausage is pushed slowly out, to drop with a thud on the floor. No one takes any notice. The girl continues working. It is exactly like a horse in a stable. Victoria pounds her linen thoughtfully. But a minute later she can hold it no more and, crouching slightly, releases her urine.

A cry resounds—"E-3. Come here!"

She kneels in front of the enormous Negress at the end of the chamber.

"If you want to piss you piss, dog of a financial whore. But you don't stop work, understand."

Victoria's wrists are held behind her back in a mammoth grip. The paddle swings before her eyes, suddenly whunks with tremendous force into her unexpecting stomach.

"GGGGARRRRHHHH!"

She lurches forward, drooling bile, fighting for breath. Only the Negress's grip on her wrists seems to hold her.

Then the paddle slaps under her hanging breasts. First it pats, then it whacks.

Victoria writhes like a worm.

"NOOOOOO!"

The paddle swats her underbreasts as if the woman were bouncing two balls on it. And when Victoria's wriggling becomes too peremptory she gets another clout in the belly, just to take her breath away.

"OOOOH . . . *mercy!*"

\* \* \*

"Ducky, let it go."

It is the quiet time of day. Evening. The last Ode to the Well-Doer has been sung. Vilma is sitting on her bed scratching her inflamed cunt. Victoria is watching with all her soul. Margot says nothing.

"If it's got to come, it's got to come," Vilma wisely advises.

There are only the four of them in the hut.

In the center stands Joy. She is dressed in her best, not her encampment shirt. It is a skimpy little body thing of blue wool under which she wears a pantygirdle, anchoring nylons, and even a slip. She is sweating and she is crying. Long slow tears course over her frightened face like smears of oil.

She is wearing a portable circular stock locked into position to hold her head and hands. It is as if she is holding up a small table on her shoulders, and indeed this is the object of the exercise. She is being trained to be a serving table. On its surface now stand two glasses of water, brimming full. Her sentence is to stand in silence like this without spilling a drop for a half hour. Her time is nearly up. Then, why does she look so wretched? Why is Victoria staring at her softly writhing legs with such attention?

For there are complications as usual. Before donning this stock Joy has been taken to the washroom and felt the cold nose of Cheeky's enema syringe stuck up her anus. Hot olive oil. Now she is desperately fighting her final last not to move her bowels.

She has to . . . she has to . . . .

She bites her lip, gazing frantically at the glasses inches from her eyes. The griping is getting ghastly and her spasms are making her tilt the stock. Oh God!

"Let it come," soothed Vilma. "Relax. Don't fight it. That's the only way you can keep on balancing them."

Victoria sees the steady flow of tears with bated breath. Joy is going to have to go. She knows it. And in her deepest self she acknowledges the expertise of this mastery. To be made to befoul one's clothes, like a child. What finer reversion . . . Joy gives a sudden stifled wail. She dips her knees, still keeping the tray vertical by a miracle of coordination. She makes a categoric sound.

"Poor kid," says Vilma softly.

Suddenly there is a shriek. One of the glasses has toppled. It falls and breaks, streaming water. Joy bursts into a panic of crying. The second glass follows suit.

Cheeky stands in the door. The girl looks at her over the edge of her stock with total terror.

"I thought I told you not to spill those glasses, swine. Water is valuable out here." The captor comes slinking forward, her helmet of hair shining. "Turn round. Ach. You've dirtied yourself, you pig." A sudden fit of sobbing and shitting doubles Joy before her then. "E-1, take her into the washroom, get her out of this thing, and hose her down after she's stripped. You, E-2, sweep up this glass, hurry." She unclips her rapier of a switch and looks at Victoria fondly. The girl is standing at attention before her bed. "You are learning, you two. You will learn even more after a morning lying in the ditch of a latrine. I intend to whip your little friend rather hard. Each time she cries out will mean a stroke for you, E-3, understand?"

Joy is brought back sobbing and dripping.

"Assume the position," she is told.

*Thwwwwlck!*

One, two, three . . . .

Victoria hears the first cry as if her soul had been sliced with the switch.

In the evening sun the six girls, Victoria and Joy among them, hang suspended against the sky at the end of the rifle range. A group of guards stand chatting about thirty yards away, loading their glistening airguns.

The six naked bodies of young girl-meat have been suspended by their wrists from a high bar. But their ankles, similarly cuffed, are stretched by chains to another bar on the ground, so taut that each body could be a bowstring. Victoria feels she can hardly breathe, so tightly are her tendons stretched. A corset would be comfortable by comparison. A last guard has just been round tensing up all these bolts and screws. And then she stops behind Victoria. The girl feels a cold touch as the brush draws over her bottom. The guard is drawing the target.

When she has finished the six bottoms of the dangling capitalist criminals have been decorated in this manner, each target circle enclosing both buttocks and embracing both in its diameter—with the anal hole as bull's eye. Victoria hears one girl whimpering in anticipation.

Desperately she clenches her buttocks, it is all she can do. The air-rifles are clicking behind, being loaded with the little silk-feathered darts she has already felt once in her hide. Each is dipped in its stinging solution first. There is much laughing and chattering in Chinese. She cannot look round, however; her neck is encased in a collar protecting the back of her head from unlikely injury. Suddenly there is a cry—it comes even before the little *pwft* of sound from the air-rifle. The bar gives a lurch.

Victoria gets her first full in the right cheek. An outer, perhaps. She is unable to repress a short sharp cry. The air is flying with the whistly little darts . . . pwfttt . . . pwfttt! She waits and waits—"OW!" Her body bounds as another thucks into her right. All six girls are gasping and bounding in their bonds. All six receive the five darts of the first round in their behinds. Then the marksmen come forward to check their scores. There is much merriment now and as each dart is checked it is pulled out of the heinie with a little dribble or ooze of blood. Joy has the highest score.

It is on the third and final round that Victoria knows she has a sure-shot. This guard is a literal devil.

*Pwfffft!*

She sinks the first of her five into the inside of Victoria's left cheek, low. A cry. It hurts hopelessly. Then the second, deep inside on the left.

"Jesus Christ help me!"

A third inside on the right. The fourth just below it, a deep worrying ache. Victoria feels her loins try to shed themselves of pain, as if on their own. The basin of her bottom opens a little . . . only slightly, but enough.

PWFFFT!

It snicks in between anus and cunt.

Prolonged scream. High A.

The six girls are let down and led off to the hospital, where the crone attends to their wounds.


"Piss!"

Victoria is standing in the center of the hut, stark naked and her hands held behind in thumb-cuffs. She has just made a twenty-minute confession of her crimes in front of her Benefactress. The three others watch from in front of their beds.

Victoria finds it hard to, with closed legs, but does.

"Now shit!"

Victoria's expression does not change. After a second she raises a knee.

"Yes?"

"May I have permission to crouch, Benefactress?"

"Go on, then."

She crouches, holding open her cheeks, and drops a small one.

Cheeky stares at it in disgust.

"A criminal capitalist turd," she says. "It's not very big. E-1, come here and produce a better specimen from your inside."

"Certainly, Benefactress. Thank you very much."

Vilma squats and exudes a simply enormous steaming sausage, dry and firm. She returns to her place. The Chinese guard pushes it beside the other, smaller offering with the toe of her thonged sandal.

"Now, E-3, get down and lick them. Lie flat on your belly on the floor and lick them. Don't eat them, but lick them lovingly until they're shiny."

Victoria blindly obeys. Flat on her tummy, her head over the excreta she licks a long tongue over the bitter surfaces, until they are wet with her saliva, and almost as glazed as her own unseeing eyes.

A foot in front Cheeky has started swinging her switch.

"Open your mouth wide, E-3, and put it over the larger one. Touch it but do not swallow or lick it. Just go down on it. If I see so much as a toothmark on that thing you're on Orders for disobedience. Now then, E-1," she says in a genial purr, letting the tail of her switch draggle over the bare bottom on the floor before her, "what am I going to do now?"

"You are going to make her open wide her legs, Benefactress," came the reply with alacrity, almost cheerfulness, from the vicinity of Vilma's bed.

"True. And then?"

"You make her arch up her criminal pelvis, so that her gangster of a pussy is on display."

"Yes, yes. And next?"

"You honor her miserable crease, Benefactress, with a stroke of the switch, as hard as it is possible to hit."

"And where does the wiry tail fetch up?"

"Either on the quim lips or on the pulpy flesh beside them."

"Will it hurt a little?"

"Hurt, Benefactress?" The voice seems full of thought, perplexed you might say. "To say it will be inconceivable agony . . . well, such words are meaningless and stream from the vocabulary of another era, a corrupt epoch. One's whole body becomes sensation. The mind is purified of all thought. When you gave me my first, Benefactress, my mouth was full of shit but I didn't taste a thing. Truly."

"Yes," said the guard dreamily. "And I had to give you another. You squirmed on the floor for three whole minutes. Open your legs, E-3, and push up your pussy . . ."

But Victoria has fainted in a slump.

The trouble with the well-built English girl tethered to the little table on her knees is that she has had no permission to faint. It is evening and outside the main hut of Eighteen A is a platoon of disciplined Algerian soldiery; they are on their way to enrailment for Israel, where they hope to wipe out all Hebrew dogs once and forever.

Under the eyes of two smiling overseers, their eyes no more than silky slits, Victoria takes a very deep breath as she lies over the table. The first soldier is coming in, his boots stamping impatiently. The first of forty-two. Fumbling at his flies. In full erection.

Victoria has been sentenced to take all forty-two, the Corporal included, in her mouth and swallow their enjoyment without losing a drop. And the trouble with this is that only after he has buggered her soundly for a bit is he empowered to shoot off in her mouth.

The presence of the two Chinese chicks in their tight blue pants excites, rather than dampens, the approaching soldier. He cones a rigid rod to the delicate sphincter ring, sees it encircled by the whitish gristle for a second, then plugs her to the hilt with a grunt. Victoria gasps.

"Uh-uh, that's enough," says one of the grinning guards and the man withdraws. The prick is fat and slimed and Victoria tastes herself as she sucks. Soon sperm boils at her tonsils, she gargles and retches but manages to swallow all. Soldier number two comes in.

This one buggers her brutally and, out of breath, she loses him in her lips at the last. The wet eye spits at her face in swift hot licks, ending up one nostril. For that clumsiness she receives three cuts. Her backside looks beautiful as it's whipped, slack, slippery, the anus oozing uneasily a trickle.

But after fifteen it fails to go fast enough.

There is a schedule to meet.

The men must double up. So Victoria is rammed from the back while she finishes off the one in her mouth. She is beginning to go dizzy and is terrified she will faint again. They all hold her so hard by the hair at the back of her head. They pump so frantically. The walls of her mouth seem coated in scum, each cock seems to steam, swallowing is an effort, semen swamps her being. She is mindless, inert as her body is banged into the side of the little table by each buggery, finally her eyes go glassy and the last man has to lave his prick on a lolling and unconscious tongue. He spills inaccurately and Victoria, awoken by three more lively slices, licks up his spurtings.

Nor is this all. She is bound on her back and two rings of gold tighten on each nipple in the manner of earrings. The gristly tips burst out of these under pressure, twin coral blobs, thick, heavy and excited-looking. A small short needle, dipped in some caustic solution, threads slowly through the bursting button. Victoria watches aghast, mewing. A big drop of blood swells and falls. The needle is left there, anchoring the ring in place. And then she truly screams, like a maniac. For they are doing the same to her clitoris.

She is returned to the hut with her hands behind her in thumb-cuffs. Left there with the others she sits on her bed as though it were made of soft eggs.

Vilma sees the spots of blood seeping at the breasts, says, "Poor sweet. Did they ring you then as well? I've had that one, too. Meant to increase the sensitivity. They'll leave 'em in till tomorrow and I tell you, it's an odd thing, it engorges and enlarges your clit. After my first even the touch of my shirt was enough to send me off. Thought it was something I'd eaten. Geez, must'a come a dozen times that morning. Is there anything I can do to help?"

For Victoria has stood up. Slowly, swaying a little, her hands behind her she makes for the washroom. Here she kneels over the canal of their excretions and is most monumentally sick. She seems to vomit the very sun from her belly, in long, hot, gusting retches. And then the most curious thing happens. The clam of her speared clit gives a definite wriggle. Oh! NO! The thing is coming but is hurting. It's hurting like hell and yet a sobbing flush of liquid lightning volts down her shuddering body. Her cunt quakes, stewing inside. Cloudy gouts pour from her quim, her clit jerks like a tongue and simply will not finish. She sits down on her beaten buttocks and says, "Oh God oh God," over and over.

And keeps on coming.

Joy is lying on her side. She has been beaten for spilling a sauce in the kitchen that morning, and doesn't want to be again. The Bottom is lined with lumpy weals.

Victoria comes over and sits behind her. Behind The Behind. Slowly stroking the satiny skin she pretends to be soothing. Slowly she leans forward and whispers in the sleepy ear and hair. Joy's violet eyes come awake. Trust Vikki. She has found a way to escape. Every day a laundry van comes up from the regiment quartered nearby; the guards go off while the girls load the sacks. They could hide under the sacks . . . .

Suddenly the hut is galvanized. The four occupants are to attention in front of their beds. Cheeky is standing there menacingly. She walks up to Victoria.

"There's going to be a public flogging. Two girls working in the laundry thought they could escape by hiding under the sacks, in back of the Army lorry. They got as far as Tipaza before we caught them. Everyone out to watch. The younger one's getting twenty-eight, and the older is getting forty-two, and most of them'll have to be across the arse 'cos with the whip she'd faint, else. I'm sorry it's not you, E-3, but one of these days." Then from the door she turns—"Both of them local kids. You may have seen them. The younger one's only thirteen. The older is fifteen. They're having their enemas now, and then their backs are treated. That whip can scar."

The captives form a square in the compound to watch. Victoria's knees might be made of aspic. Joy wants to wee-wee badly. In the center stands a sort of gibbet. Surely they aren't going to hang the girls, are they? Guards encircle this wooden dais, making last adjustments. Amongst them the grinning mammoth of the laundry Overseer, in khaki tunic skirt, her larded upper body bare. She is oiling a thin hard whip, rumored to be of lizardskin, its last six inches braided with fishing twine, yet extremely lean—a lock of eel-like leather that looks as if it could cut into a stone. No capitalist criminal sees it without a shudder in the guts. Victoria stares stonily. She has lost all identity at this moment.

Equality Hut is leashed together by throat collars and a tinkling chain that threads through their thumb cuffs in back. Their bottoms are warm under the tails of their shirts, but they are all goosing at the thought of punishment. There but for the grace of God . . . .

Animation. The doors of the main hut open and the procession emerges to clanging cymbals. Twice the two culprits, buck bare but for high dunce's hats, each with DESERTER on it in blood-red letters, circle the square behind the tall girl with the clashing cymbals. They end up under the gibbet. There the Well-Doer addresses them.

He does so in Arabic. For the pair are two Sudanese lambs being sold as virgins. The speaker system announces their crimes then in French, English, and German. Then their sentences.

The thirteen-year-old is taken first. A delicious, dark-haired morsel with two satiny plaits, when the dunce's cap drops off. She contrasts with the Negress who draws her forward as if the two had come from separate races. The girl is like a boy. She is lean and lissom, with a pitiful spineless back through which the pebbles of her vertebrae push, and whose amber skin shines a little since it has been painted for the occasion with a collodium solution to prevent deep scarring.

Under the high gibbet she kneels with feet apart. Her buttocks are sloping, feline and unmarked, their skin as if transparent, a sheen behind which someone holds a flame. The deep groove bisecting these sweet jellyish eggs is ambery velvet also. She kneels and holds up her manacled hands now. These are secured to a cord at the top of the gibbet. With her legs strapped fast at knee and ankles she is then hauled until her torso is drum-taut, the ribs protruding. The Negress stands back with the whip. Its tip trails in the dust and flickers like

*145*

a serpent. Surely it will slice this fragile adolescent in two.

*A crack like a pistol-shot!*

But the girl makes no move. The whip-plait was popped inches off her arse. The Negress was taking aim. The Well-Doer nods and makes a finger signal. Suddenly all know that the gibbet is wired to the speaker. Everything is to be heard magnified.

The lazy tail performs a semi-circle, gathering speed as it moves. There comes a desolating flick as the very tip bites. A large gasp ululates across the compound. A razor has slashed across the liquid rump. The thin red line exudes spicules of pure ruby on the right.

The buttocks are accorded three, a punishment in itself from all appearances. The next two are under the shoulders, the tip whipping freshily into the right armpit. The girl jerks and cries shrilly. Two a little lower down, and then two more lower still, just above her waist. These seem to fetch her terribly. She writhes like a dervish, filling the air with her exaggerated gasps, while the hospital crone bathes her face and holds restoratives to her shining nostrils. She has had nine—less than a third of her sentence—and her breath labors like a dying warrior's.

At a sign from the Well-Doer the buttocks are now treated to four, low down. Then the back. The girl is barred almost from neck to knees. She takes all twenty-eight fully conscious and after it is over lies in the dust at the side, her legs dimly threshing, her halved arse bloody, leaking into the slice of sex beneath.

The fifteen-year-old has to be secured forcibly. She is whimpering, in a frenzied panic of pure terror. But when the cuts begin something comes together in her soul; she bears the blows remarkably, twisting but not crying much. It is more a long moaning lament, from start to finish. She is repeatedly given restoratives.

Her buttocks are treated first, too. They are thicker and solider, yet bleed more into the bargain. Ten are put across them, then six down the back. Ten again on the buttocks, six on the back. There are ten more to come.

They are incredible strokes. The whipmistress lifts the body of each one. The air fills with screeches. Every drop of color is drained from the faces of the watching prisoners. Victoria thinks she sees blood fairly spray at one shot.

After it is over the dunce's caps are replaced and the two offenders have to sit astride two notched bars, with their legs held apart by further bars beneath them. The bar eats into their pussies and anal canals deeply. The whole camp is paraded past them.

"Come here, E-4. What do you want most in life?"

"After the dictatorship of the proletariat, and long life for Chairman Mao, I would like something that was a sign of your attention, Benefactress."

"Such as?"

Joy does not have to think. She says instantly, "Like a whipping, or . . . or being able to touch or taste, or smell, something that has been close to you. To remind me of my unworthy presence."

"Something that has been inside me, perhaps?"

"That would be almost too great a favor, Benefactress."

"You're right. It would. Besides I want to beat you."

"Thank you, Benefactress."

"This time it's going to be on the breasts. The undersides. So make yourself comfortable lying on the bed with your top over the side and your pears dangling down. Like you saw with Margot yesterday."

"Yes, Benefactress. Thank you."

# 11

BUYERS CAME FOR THEM, OF COURSE.
There were two burly Chinese who looked like Kansas businessmen in their neat suits and hand-painted ties. They wanted to see Margot whipped and did, in the hut.

A strange shy Western woman was ushered in by two guards one day. Vilma had to go under her skirt and perform. But she was not sold.

Then one sunny "rest" afternoon the Arab came who bought The Bosom and The Bottom. His eyes above the veiling reminded Victoria of the man who had helped them in the airplane. But she could not be sure. He felt them all over like animals, went away and then Cheeky came back to tell them.

They were slaves.

At last they left the compound for a comfortable limousine; the Arab sat in front beside a uniformed chauffeur. The girls were in their Sunday best, holding their handbags on their knees. The car took them to a beaten strip of land on which an airplane waited. Some tiny moth.

Evidently a private plane, with seats for some dozen. They taxied off, alone with the man in the cockpit whose crewcut looked somehow assuring. When they were aloft he shouted back, "Comfortable?"

"Are there any pillows, cushions, you know?"

"Only those in front of you, doll. Ever hear the one about Ding Dong Bell?"

Only Marshall, Victoria was thinking, tells that kind of . . . then she was standing up, holding to one seat and plucking weakly at Joy in front of her. For the man had on large dark glasses and was hardly in profile, but the man they were with was Marshall Dexter.

"Great Scott," cried Victoria, striding unsteadily into the cockpit (Joy followed with more softish bumps beside her), "I never thought I'd be glad to see *you*."

"Marshy!" wailed Joy, and threw her arms about his neck.

"Steady the Buffs," grinned Marshall Dexter happily.

For several seconds his face seemed drowned in breasts.

"But, Joy ducky, look. There are our other bags. The ones with the money—and our proper papers."

She stared in puzzlement at the pilot's feet.

"So it was you stole our panties, Mr. Dexter. Hm. But this bag here, this one I left with a man called Mémé Pizziani. At Antibes. He provided us with the false papers we're carrying now. What an operator."

Slowly, with a Hemingwayesque shrug. Marshall Dexter smiled—"Mémé works for me."

"He . . . works . . . for . . ." Victoria grandly straightened. "Marshall, where are you taking us? Put us down this minute."

"I'm rescuing you, stupid, don't you understand?"

"You can't be. We've just been sold."

"Which is to say bought."

"What's going on here?" said Joy, getting lost.

*150*

"I've bought you."

"How can you have? And what's all this about Mémé Pizziani working for . . . but that was the question we . . ."

"Thanks for not telling them, Vi dear. Ibrahim has long had a yen to use our guts as spaghetti. If he knew us."

"But you never had a cent," said Joy.

"No, but I have lots and lots of lovely francs," said Marshall, making a dive. "You could say, several million." Then he added as they straightened, "Funny thing, this Aunt Grizel of yours. I said I'd fetch you for her. You can have tomorrow shopping in Algiers, if you like, but I did promise to put you on the plane for her day after that."

They stayed in the relative luxury of the Aletti, where the first thing both girls did was to have a long hot tub. Several hours and many martinis later they were dining on a terrace with Marshall.

Dreamily, a little muzzily, Victoria put a hand on his shoulder; and the youth who fought bulls in Spain on the side looked at it as if it were some landed fish. One he had been longing to land ever since he'd seen it, in fact.

"Marshy darling, how long were we in that awful concentration camp? Like, how many months, I mean?"

"Months! You were there six days, that's all."

"Six days!" said Joy.

"I don't understand," said Victoria.

Then suddenly something cleared, she smiled divinely and said—"But I'm beginning to."

The man smiled with her. He knew he had it made.

Aunt Grizel was grizzled. At fifty-three her short still-dark hair might have been flicked with streaks of accented grey, but her body was more that of a boy's.

She was an ex-country golf champion with a yen for exercise. She did a pitiless set of setting-up exercises after her cold tub each morning.

She met the two girls at Nice airport that sunny afternoon in a trim triacetate three-piece whose body skirt kept its body, and matched their own for length.

To their dismay, the girls soon learned that Aunt Grizel was more than accurately informed as to their adventures.

In the woman's sumptious hotel rooms both girls were rather formally admonished, and, to their horror, somewhat less formally thrashed raw by a fiendishly crackling Aunt Grizel, wielding the Birch like a champion.

More sore than ever, the girls were speeded home.

# 12

VICTORIA ARRIVED BACK AT THE FAMILY ESTATE the following afternoon. She was fetched in an antiquated, and quite unnecessary, pony-trap by a senile groom, called—of all things—Groome. It was of course pouring with filthy rain.

He set her down in the stable-yard and helped carry her few things in solicitously. Most of one bag was money. Victoria doffed her brass-buttoned maxi-coat and exposed herself in a cannon-red mini, whose soft gathered skirt ceded to pantyhose of cocoa cream. The groom's eyes sharpened at the hint of the opaque part of these.

"Yer father and mother just bin out riding, Miss. I rather thinks as yer father wants to see yer."

"Thanks, Groome," she said, dropping a tip into his ready palm. He gazed at it aghast. It was a fiver, a pony! His rheumy eyes followed the limber and liquid movement of those girlish limbs, that bouncy butt beneath the flippy skirt. Many was the time he had peeked through the dairy keyhole at the backside getting its bit as a kid. He would give half that five-pound note in his right hand to see the same again.

Millicent, Victoria's mother, came out of a morning-room in checked vest and riding breeches, carrying some flowers. She gave her rather apprehensive daughter the merest of pecks on the cheek and said in a *distrait* way, "I believe your father wants to see you in his study, child." She added, "Before we go any further."

She vanished round a passage corner.

The last Earl of Wrenche stood before his fireplace and family portraits, betweeded, booted, and in steaming breeches, quaffing a glass of port. He had to beat back a pair of horsehair mustaches to do so. The room, his den, was truly one—being largely furnished with old stuffed animal heads, antlers, foxes' brushes and the like. In one corner, by the sporting prints, stood two twelve-bore shotguns, a broken tennis racquet, three croquet mallets, a cricket bat, much bound, and three long lean yellow canes. It was at the last of these that he was looking as his lovely daughter entered.

"Hello, Daddy. Sorry I got back a trifle late. We . . . got into some difficulty. Actually."

She had been about to approach and kiss him (the Earl administered kisses you felt for a fortnight), but the look in his eye deterred her. She stayed where she was, trailing a leg and twisting in her fingers a handkerchief the size of a postage stamp.

"I'm not going to ask where you've been, m'dear. But I suppose you know you're over two weeks late for School."

"Yes, Daddy, like I said. We . . . that is, Joy and myself . . . got into a little difficulty. It wasn't our fault at all. Really."

"I'm not asking questions and I'm not expecting any answers. I'm just going to discourage your doing the same again. Ever. Your mother and I were extremely worried about you. I'm going to give you the hiding of your life."

"Ber-but . . ." Victoria's mouth dropped wide. This she hadn't been expecting. Her throat went very dry. "But please, Daddy. Aunt Grizel gave us both a jolly tight caning. In Nice."

"You're going to get another now."

"But, Daddy, please. It was only yesterday. And it will . . . oh my God, it will hurt abominably, I'm all bruised there, and . . ." Tongue whipping over her lips, Victoria felt butterflies up her tummy. Adapting another tone of voice she said evenly, "It won't be possible for me to be corporally chastised today, I'm afraid."

"Why? Got the curse?" The last Earl charged round his desk and drew from his favorite corner his favorite cane, a lovely long silky hickory that made Victoria feel weak to look at—it was his longest and lithest. A cold sweat started in the region of her shoulderblades. His Army cane. "Used to take this one to lazy drummer-boys," said the Earl with relish, cutting the air as though it were flannel. "Sliced the fat off 'em by inches. When's the last time you felt this, my beauty?"

"Last holidays. And I get beaten all the time at school."

"Not enough, it seems. You're a big girl now, with a nice big bum; you're going to get it moving and follow me to the dairy and I'm going to put this across you as I never have before."

"Please . . . *Daddy* . . ."

But the irate Earl had stormed past her and following, half at a run, Victoria felt jelly in her loins. A faintness behind her eyes. Out through a side-door, down the covered way to the outhouses, across some cobbles in the soaking rain and into the dreaded dairy. The place of her domestic discipline since she cared to remember. Which wasn't very long.

There was nothing in the dairy, except for an odd milk-can or two. A step, a drain, a sink, it was all of stone and functional and bare. The Earl shut the door and fiddled with a rope hanging from a pulley in the ceiling.

Victoria tried her unsteady last (the *length* of that fiendish cane . . . after all, she wasn't a drummer-boy, was she?)—"Daddy, please . . . I'm grown up now."

"My girl," quoth the Earl in his wrath, "I'm going to tan your taffy hide till you're married. Whereupon I trust your husband will keep up the good work."

"But I'm beastly wealed behind," quavered Victoria. "It's going to hurt like billyho on Aunt Grizel's."

"If I have anything to do with it, it is. Now stop talking and drop your britches." He added gruffly, "Hose 'n' all."

"But, Daddy, you can't . . . on the bare, I mean. After all I'm seventeen."

"And seventeen's what I mean to give you," roared the Earl triumphantly. "One for each year of your life."

"With that cane?" said Victoria faintly, gulping. "You must be joking." But she knew he wasn't. She stalled heuristically—"My panties won't protect me any, honest. They're . . . they're of acetate rayon encron."

"Of what?"

"It doesn't matter." She raised a leg to lift them off. "I'll do it," she said, picking up the ritual two clothespegs of their tradition and pinning her skirt up with them. Hoseless, she put her hands behind her back.

"I like to see my strokes falling," said the Earl, his eyes sharpening. "Where they fall, I mean." He harrumphed heartily, feeling his prick jerk at his loins.

"I say, Grizel did mark ye up a bit, didn't she?" He snapped the equally ritual handcuffs, a guard-room variety, on his daughter's wrists behind her.

"This can't be happening," said Victoria dimly. "You can't possibly be going to give me seventeen on a sit-upon as sore as mine."

"She didn't hit full across," said the Earl, bending and inspecting. "Though this must have been a juicy one, heh."

The rope dropped from the ceiling had a clip. It clipped to Victoria's manacles and drew her arms painfully behind her back, bending her over, head down. The Earl ran one end of the rope round a wall-hook only when she was on tiptoe.

"I'd forgotten this position," said Victoria. "Sometimes, in nightmares, I really think it's the worst."

"I also like my meat wet," said the Earl in businesslike tone, taking up a sponge used for cleaning cars, filling it with water from a tap and squeezing it out over his daughter's bottom. Victoria shivered, she always found this part of the childhood ritual particularly degrading and anxious-making, somehow. "Hurts twice as much wet," said the Earl. He took up his endless cane.

"Daddy, I have a confession to make."

"What is it now?"

"I'm so bloody frightened I'm afraid I'm going to pee. If you hit me quickly . . . aaaah," she hissed as the helpless hot jet struck between her strained and arching toes. "Ooooh," she gasped, blushing crimson. "I'm ser-ser-sorry, I've never done that before."

"Doesn't matter. Groome will swab it down."

Good old Groome, she thought hysterically—bowed over, watching through the keyhole, with his streaming yellow eyes. "May I bite on the rope?"

Then, after that, gripping between her teeth the lump

of cord that helped her not to cry out and thus satisfy the masturbating stable-boys, she was ready for it. In her red mini, exposing her tautly clefted, striated buttocks, Victoria was really ready for it. There came the Earl's thudding rush of a run and the first stroke sent her swinging, grunting, forward. He hit as hard as he could. Liquid flame lashed across her fanny.

"YYYNNNNNG!"

How she ever got through it, she never knew.

The strokes were so severe the Earl could keep her at a pinnacle of pain with only three a minute. She squirmed and spun like some landed trout. Lost footing, found it, doubled up a leg, moaning, at some particularly lancinating stroke. The Earl prided he did this work as he did all—with vigor. By the time he had finished that once-creamy vision of a posterior was a flaming cauldron of thick purple weals, at least two of which were bleeding. Releasing the rope was the part he enjoyed. Victoria lay squirming like a cut worm on her side, gasping for breath. It was a very satisfactory spectacle, indeed, and excited him as nothing else. This time she gratified him with some doublings and thigh-threshings that sent his cock sentry-high.

"Now get dressed, and let that be a lesson to you."

Victoria did so in a daze. Never, never . . . .

"And send your mother to me."

"Mother?"

She groped her way out, one hand on the wall and one on what seemed to be her severed seat.

The Earl gave his prick a vigorous rub.

When his wife entered five minutes later he was thoroughly ready for her.

"You sent for me, dear?"

Millicent Wrenche was a tall, good-looking woman in her forties; a good, long sloping bottom filled her riding breeches to repletion, a fact not unobserved at this moment by the noble Earl.

"I did, Millie, yes. I just had to flog Vikki."

"I know. I saw her. I hope you weren't too severe." She looked at him with wondering dark eyes and then looked down. "Did Victoria forget her manners so much as to lose her water?"

"Yep. Skinned her on the right side a trifle, but she'll be right as rain in two ticks. I think she hurt herself writhing on the floor afterwards almost as much as during."

They laughed together.

"You really do know how to cane a woman, darling."

"A woman?" The Earl's eyes narrowed.

"Well, a girl."

"And that's the thing, m'dear. Why I asked you to see me here, actually. Now I think that you and I have always been even-stephens in everything, heh? Never ask of one what one wouldn't of another, heh. Except of others only what you'd take yourself . . ."

The woman's eyes went vague. "I don't get your meaning, dear."

"This. It's that I've always felt the bringing up of our gel to be your responsibility, Millie. You know that. Oh, true I've whacked her ass a few times, but it was usually on your instigation. Now, this last delinquency . . . a serious matter . . . very . . . I view it . . . as reflecting . . . on *you*." The Earl's breath came stertorous. He took another deep one. "To tell the truth," he got out bluntly, "you deserve what she got. Millie mine, I'm asking you to take a hiding. With this." And he grimly flexed the cane.

There was a long silence in the dairy. You could almost have heard Groome panting outside.

Finally the woman went up to him with a dark, dewy look in her great grave eyes.

"You . . . want . . . to . . . give . . . me . . . the stick?"

"Across the bottom."

There was another long pause. The Earl's heart was pounding fiercely.

For his fair wife's fingers were moving slowly but certainly on her belt, the fly-front of her breeches—which were now hanging absurdly at her knees, over her boots. As were her . . . panties! She was naked from checked vest to boot-tops and she had absolutely superb, long, oval, pear-shaped, rich-looking, well-downed, close-clefted and fatly overhung . . . his own mouth dropped open.

"How many did Vikki get? It looked as if you'd cut right through her to me."

"Seventeen. You needn't take as many."

She shook her head slowly. "I'm afraid I need." She looked at him slowly. Then gave her right cheek a solid wallop that jounced it. "Now, my dear. I want you to take these ignorant, sulky buttocks and cut them with that cane just as hard as you jolly well can. Make me squeal like a pig if you like, but so help me God I won't be satisfied until I feel them twice their weight and I'm begging to be crucified rather than you continue the treatment. And at that point I want you to slice them as you would a side of ham, only nice and low, where it hurts most, and take your time, I want six to start me off, all up and down the breadth of them, and then a dozen very slowly, making eighteen in all, and," she paused, a trifle wildly gasping, "about the last dozen I want to know nothing at all. Except that I've reached heaven."

The Earl had heard this speech agog, mouth drooping.

"Then, Millie, you mean I can?"

"It's what I've been aching for all our married life."
"Millicent!"
"Darling!"

Less than eighty miles away, in another part of that cold county where the rain lashed on windowpanes, cascaded into water-spouts and sent tweeded citizens in off the streets with wet doggy smells about them, another culprit in crime was faring no more favorably.

Joy ffrenche stood most disconsolately fingering the border of her "Baby-Buttoner" sweaterling, her only super-shape insurance this day, really no more than a longish stone-colored cardigan, under which she wore a bra and garterless girdle, a whisperthin nothing of lycra spandex powernet that was having some trouble in enclosing The Bottom.

"But you can't be going to give me a whipping, Mother," she was saying between gulps, "I only just got one. Please."

"Can't I just," said her mater, an energetic woman in tartan slacks and a cashmere sweater who was making dreadful preparations on the floor with certain bolts and nuts and bits of solid wood. "Want to take a bet? Unshaven armpits, indeed."

They were in the so-called playroom of the house, a large, and largely bare, parquet expanse, furnished with the apparatus of domestic discipline where Mrs. ffrench-Fox-Todde reigned supreme and brought up her daughter "the hard way." Her violet eyes already swimmy, Joy looked anything but about to play.

"Please, Mother, please." Instinctively, as if on their own, her hands felt back under her little skirtlet behind; her large and lovely chubbies felt fatter than ever, quivering with fear, and hotly lined. "Please. Aunt Grizel gave us twice nine. It was absolute agony."

"Can't help that, m'dear," came the reply. She had arranged the little oaken plank over which her daughter would bend vertically now, to her satisfaction, and stood up, dusting off her hands. She was a good big woman, a little on the heavy side, who had given that Swedish look to Joy. There was weight in her cuts and she knew it. She was going to enjoy every moment of this, and write it in her memory for ever.

"Come, my dear, you have nothing to lose but your girdle."

"Mother, *please*. Isn't there anything I can do to stop you whipping me again? I got twice nine . . . eighteen awful strips across my bottom only yesterday. And, and Aunt Grizel hits like anything. My whole bum is lined and sore. Especially the . . . lower part."

"That's going to make what I give you hurt so much more, isn't it, pet."

Joy's bosom rose and fell. Tears welled from her eyes. She was the very picture of apprehension and her mother drank it in, deep.

"Th-that . . . thing you use on me . . . is so horrible."

"It's going to be worse than that today. Come on, take it all off, and show me the funny little lines on your body you're complaining of. Let's see if we can't add just a few carbons."

But the girl couldn't move. A hand flashed out and rang her head like a bell.

"Ow!"

"Come to your senses, girl," seethed her mother through her teeth then. "I'm going to teach you to run around putting it out for every Tom, Dick and Harry— and mostly Tom—on the South Coast of France. How many pricks did you have up your twat? Eh, eh? Shameless hussy, what would have happened if you'd run out of the pill? Did you know you can't get it there?

You don't seem to realize, my dear, I'm going to have a quarter of an hour in here making you feel about as sorry for yourself as you've ever felt, slowly. There's nothing you can do about it and if you go on stalling I'll make it longer. Now then. Every stitch off. I haven't birched your bottom on top of a previous beating, and it ought to be salutory. Strip."

The blubbering girl did as bid. Truly she was a jelly of terror already. But when she turned it was to find her inexorable mother facing her wearing now a pair of black leather gardening gloves. She seized one wrist in entreaty.

"Mother, *pleeeease*. Not the nettles. Please. My God," she sank to one knee, "I'm your daughter, aren't I? You can't want to be as cruel as that. To be birched . . . on top of a nettling . . . it's, ough, it's the worst I know . . . ug . . . ug . . . ug." She collapsed in a flurry of crying.

Mrs. ffrench-Fox-Todde watched this symptomatology of the damned with inner delight. She was seething all over now. Ants were crawling up her spine. In her small conservatory she had a culture of West Indian devil's nettles. The leaf was not jagged like the English garden variety, it was purplish when mature and could sting through a man's trousers. What's more the ampoules lasted an hour, increasing in their wicked sting if rubbed in. Which, with the birch, they were.

"Have you quite finished, child? Aunt Grizel marked you nicely, I see. It will be a pleasure to work you where she began. Come now. Pull yourself together and try to show some courage. Play up School."

The words drew Joy out of her semi-consciousness of terror. She went to where her mother was standing and spread her legs widely.

Mrs. Todde liked a certain amount of reaction when nettling. It was good for the victim's soul to see it

*163*

herself, too. Joy was simply secured to ring-bolts spraddlelegged, with her hands fixed in cuffs behind her. She could—and would—stretch on tiptoes and bend her knees, but that was all. She looked on aghast as her mother selected a bunch of the purple leaves from a vase at the side and holding them gingerly approached her back.

"Now then, Miss Cunty Kate, let's see how you like the kiss of the devil."

"Hou . . . *ou!*" cried Joy immediately.

The woman paraded the nettles first up the insides of the thighs, and Joy called out at once. The edge of each leaf drew up angry white blotches, like large mosquito stings. Joy jerked and clenched, twisting.

"Whew . . . how they sting . . . moooother, pleeeeeaze!"

Her buttocks were next, each creamy cheek carefully gone over, and where the weals were the poison of the leaf was such it actually dimmed the anger of the red. Joy hissed and crouched. Her mother gently and tenderly drew the bunch of stinging leaves up her furrow—and the girl straightened with a scream.

"*That* make your twat nice and itchy, darling? Would you like some on the breasts?"

"Noooo . . . eeeeeiyeeeh!"

Her toes curled. She reared, bending her knees, and this time Mrs. Todde actually had time for a good scrubbing rub of the bloated vulval fig thrust back. Joy yelled, jacking straight.

"OOOOOOOH! Mother. This is *torture*."

"Now for the great divide."

"No, nooooh!"

Clenching her cheeks in desperation, Joy tried to look back as her mother opened the buttock cleft with finger and thumb of her left hand and widened the insides of The Bottom for application of the searing leaf.

"You disgusting girl," she said, looking at the well-sunk anal crater, "I do believe you've been buggered. Yes, that's a buggered bunghole if ever I've seen one. Just for that, I'll get some new leaves. There won't be an inch of you, either, from waist to knees that hasn't been stung by the time I've finished. And I do mean inside and out." She laughed as she began her work anew. "Darling, really, you don't have to make like a belly-dancer."

It was an excruciating business, but one judged necessary to the complete administration of correction. When it was over Joy wore a veil of blotches over both buttocks and well down each thigh, and she regaled her inexorable mother with a raging dance of pain when released, unable to refrain from rubbing at the blisters and so making them sting the more.

"Ou . . . ow . . . augh . . . it's unbearable . . . mother, mother, let me off . . . ho . . . hou . . . *aieeee!*"

"Don't show off, dear," said the good woman, shucking her cashere sweater and revealing strong breasts hammocked in an aertex bra. "And what on earth did you do the backs of your hands? Those scabs, I mean? Did you get them playing in the sand? Come here and kneel over."

Jellyish, a-blubber, the girl came forward on cat feet. She had to kneel, as always, on that awful plank, to which her ankles were strapped, well parted, then her knees. The fronts of her thighs were absolutely vertical against the board set up there, over which she duly had to bend and reach right forward, her wrists being secured in front. Worst of all was the way her mother drew two armpit straps so tight her whole chest was forced down to the flooring; this made her back arch up, thrust out . . . oh she was hopelessly on display—from behind. Joy looked sickly round as her mother went resolutely to a closet. She drew out of it a shining birch and Joy shuddered with all of herself, but particularly The Bottom.

"What a boon it was that your younger brother developed the hobby of model airplane building, dear," said the approaching ogress of her implacable parent, whisking the six or seven strands.

For the birch was shining since it was of steel. It consisted of needle-thin steel strands, used by her beastly brother in constructing rotten planes. The holding end was bound with wire and the tips soldered slightly to increase their wrap and whip. A venomous instrument, its look made Joy goose and shiver; it would be worse than, than Ali's martinet on her nettled, blotchy bum.

"How many, mother, please?"

The grim answer took the last of the poor girl's strength.

"You're getting three dozen, my love, and three down the center after. With plenty of time to reflect. And if that doesn't straighten you up, my pet, it'll be double the dose next time. Yes, six dozen across that big fat . . ."

"Mother—nooooo!"

*Zzzzzzisch!*

The steel claws whistled down, fanging that puppy flesh most cruelly. Thin streamed weals, purplish-black, dashed up as the woman whipped on. The swollen buttocks labored deliciously. The lithe tough limbs chewed into the skin. The girlish knees beat desperately with each blow, blood flecked the floor by ten.

She was cut into but not deeply; the knowing tormentress wanted only a surface rawness for the maximum of nervous sting. She played her rod low but let it lap well round, and by twenty half The Bottom was grazed and blue. From now on each stroke could be made an ordeal, and would be made so, had Mrs. ffrench-Fox-Todde anything to do with it. She was feeling extremely excited, indeed.

"Oooooh . . . mother, it's agony . . . you don't know . . ."

The telephone rang.

"Yes," she answered briskly, picking it up, if panting a trifle, "I can take it here. Who's this? Muriel . . . yes . . . yes . . . actually I am, rather . . . I'm flogging my daughter . . . mmn, Joy . . . birch, three doz . . . yes, I'm at twenty . . . no, no, doesn't seem to be enjoying it one ounce . . . still, spare the rod, I fear." She gave a gurgling chuckle. "And three down the you-know-what, after . . . Yes, I'm working low, all right . . . 'drew' at ten or so . . . from now on in, it's going to be fun. Bye, Muriel."

WHUWHUWHU—

"Mother!"

—uippp!

"AOW!"

The dry tips nipped and nicked.

How she ever got through it Joy never knew. And then her mother was standing a-straddle in front of her head.

"NOOOOOOOOO!" she screamed.

A growling man's voice came down to them after a moment—"What the devil are you two doin' in there, hey? Stickin' a pig or something?"

"Not to worry, dear," answered the woman cheerily, "it'll all be over soon."

"NOOOOOOOOOOOOOOO!" screamed Joy.

The bloody tips lagged down her central cleft, touching in measuring aim the slickly budded morsel that was her most in life.

"Ibrahim!" she yelled.

"What," said her mother thoughtfully, raising high

her steely twigs, "don't say you've been consorting with Orientals, too! Well, this is going to hurt you very considerably, m'dear. Can't help it but I have a feeling it'll remind you to keep your cunt closed and to yourself for a while."

And she lashed that sweetest self.

The Headmistress of Bothington College looked up pleasantly from behind her pince-nez the following evening. The two girls standing meekly before her were really very beautiful. And very rich. Little did she know how much so.

"Won't you both sit down?"

"We'd rather stand," said both.

"I suppose you two know," she said in the same amicable tone with which she had greeted them back, "you're over two weeks late for term."

"Yes, Head," said Victoria in her best impersonation of a remorseful voice. She plucked at her skinny mini.

"I know, Head," agreed Joy.

"Well," beamed their interlocutor, "I suppose you also know that means a mandatory public birching."

There was a sudden, sickening silence in the study. You could have heard a bobby-pin drop, and Joy dropped one.

Victoria paled visibly under her glossy tan.

"We have both already been dealt with by our parents, Head," she said as steadily as she could.

The woman nodded in agreement. "So I understand. I have been in touch with them, both. I put my point of view that I can't afford for the reputation of the School . . ."

"Play up School," said Joy.

"Play up School," said Victoria.

". . . that I can't afford to overlook this matter entirely. However, in the circumstances, I have agreed to remit a public swiping in Great Hall and let you off with a good stout caning in the gym."

In the deathly still Joy's aghast gulp sounded like a falling stone. The falling stone of her heart.

"A ker-caning?" echoed Victoria, as if ununderstanding.

"Yes. Surely you've heard of the term." The Head, pince-nez winking, continued to beam at them like some beacon. "A length of wood is applied firmly to your bent bottom. Quite hard, as a rule."

"But . . . we've just ber-ber-been . . . rather often, as it happens . . ."

"Well, another application won't do you any harm. Drive the lesson home. Two weeks is two weeks."

"Headmistress," bravely quavered Victoria then, "would you like me to expose . . . show to you . . . my posterior . . . or that of Joy?"

"That won't be necessary," was snapped back. "I've already seen it, thanks."

"Not in its present state you haven't, Ma'am. Yesterday," and bravely she fought back the rising tears, "yer-yesterday my father flogged my behind seventeen times with a miltary cane as hard as he could. It was raving frightful *agony,* Ma'am."

"And I," broke in Joy, not to be outdone, "it was three dozen with the birch. And then three down, down . . ." Her voice tailed off. The inexorable Head was still smilingly shaking her head.

"I'm sorry, girls . . ."

"I'm black and blue," said Victoria hotly. "I can't sit down comfortably and even the touch of my clothes . . ."

"Pull yourself together, Victoria," came the crisp command, accompanied by a rap of a ruler. "You're going to need all your courage in a minute. As the elder, and ringleader in the affair, I am ordering you eighteen with the cane, one more than you got yesterday and one for each day of absence. Joy will have fifteen. Matron will see to you afterwards, in the case of any serious contusions." She sighed and consulted her timepiece. "Prep has been over these ten minutes now. Miss Nicholson is awaiting you in the gymnasium."

"Ber-but I'm a Prefect," objected Victoria, lost and knowing it.

"With the Duty Prefect of the day by her side."

The grey bun of hair bowed. Without knowing what they were doing the two girls curtseyed and left. They began to trail hand in hand down the lonely long walk to the west wing. The wind howled outside. A small girl in a green tunic hurried past, rubbing her bottom and gasping loudly.

"I can't take fer-fifteen," said Joy, dragging her feet. They were almost there by now. In fact, they faced the door.

"And to think we have enough bread between us to buy this lousy dump," Victoria added in a petulant snarl.

"You don't happen to have any morphine handy, do you, Vikki?"

"Oh it was all your fault from the start," came the retort. "You lost our panties in Ste. Maxime. If it hadn't been for that. I shall enjoy seeing you get it."

"As per," said Joy wistflly. "Are you going to knock?"

"Why not?"

The gym they entered seemed brightly lit and filled entirely with—the horse. Beside it Sandra ("Sandy") Nicholson, trim in tennis attire, was cheerfully swishing the longest cane in the world. She was looking forward to thrashing an Earl's daughter.

"Good evening, Miss Nicholson," said Victoria.

"I'll take you first," said the mistress gloatingly. "Remove your pants."

"I haven't got any on," said Victoria coldly. "Pantyhose. Fifty-five shillings at Marshal and Snelgrove."

"Take them right off, replace your shoes and let's get your buttocks bare. I'm going to have to take you two down a peg . . . or two. You're about to be beaten for returning to school late. Have you anything to say?"

"Are you serious?"

"Don't be cheeky, Victoria." She waited a minute, then tapped with her wand, "Have you anything to say?"

"I . . . her-have . . . a *hell* of a ler-lot to s-s-s-saay," began Victoria, sticking out her obstinate little chin. When her rather snub face writhed up, the words were seized with choking, and the Hon. Victoria Digby was reduced to a blubbering schoolchild before them, tucking her skirt up in her belt. "I've . . . been . . . ner-nothing but beaten," she got out through sobs, "for two days running now. First, eighteen . . . ther-then seventeen . . . you don't know what it's like . . . my whole behind is bruised and if there's an ounce of fairness in this damn place you'll give them to me across the back of the legs, and, and I'll do my best to take it."

"Eighteen strokes," announced the mistress curtly. "Bend her over."

Victoria felt a tap on her shoulder. Automatically she turned as if to say icily, I don't believe I've had the pleasure of . . . .

"Hello, Victoria," said Helen Elstir.

Still sniffling, the girl was splayed across the horse, her legs very widely parted. When the trifling apology of a skirt had been drawn further up her back, even Miss Nicholson gave pause.

"Better hold her hand," she instructed her Prefect.

Happy to oblige, Helen Elstir twisted Victoria's glossy arms behind her back and straddled her head in front of the horse, gripping it between her thighs which were very muscular indeed. She did not have on panties.

Victoria felt, rather than heard, the juicy swish of air behind her, then a flame of agony sucked at her body— a vibrating stroke lashed across her bottom. On the bruised flesh a furious swollen weal sprang up.

"Oh!" she said plaintively, her cry lost in the depths of Helen Elstir's underbum.

"One," called the Prefect calmly above her.

The punishment continued. Victoria flung her legs about. Helen's snatch was wet on her nape. She tried to shake her head. At the third she hissed hotly upward—"You don't have to wank off on the back of my neck, you bitch."

But it was lost in the scant folds of the regulation tunic skirt. She twisted her head to try to bite a buttock. But in vain.

*Thwwwwlckkk!*

The punishment continued, as punishments have to.

God, as the saying went at Bothington, was always right.

From the side Joy watched the blood-blue welts piteously thicken and lumpen on the in-cringing skin, and suddenly, quite calmly, in her best tea-table, scones-and-butter tone of voice she said calmly, "What are you doing?"

At which everyone grew very much smaller. She only just got through the door in time and out.

"Come back, come back," she heard their voices of children at play calling urgently behind her. "Come back, we can't go on without you."

But she was brushing crumbling things aside, like

collapsing walls and one mirror of water, petulantly pushing at the sky (it ripped like so much scenic fabric), saying petulantly, "Mummy, mummy, they were beating a girl in there."

"Giving her a good hiding, eh?" said a woman's voice waggishly.

But they had done it, right enough. And those to whom cruelty is done will do cruelty back. Cruelty has not to do with love. Joy had to do with love. A child with weighed-down head and bones peeping through pale skin and round exposed knees is told sternly, by the stern voice of the social mentor, "I shall see you later," or "Report to me in my study." As he escapes through the woods beyond the masquerade, the prison staff looks on and jeers. Pitiless, perilous names are thrown out like chaff. Only the child with torn hair knows that the stage is flawed. Its gasping life is love. Out of terror it makes ecstasy.

Joy walked on in the greenest grasses. She asked no quarter. As the fox knows its den she hears always a child crying a name all night—and the name was love, the name was love . . . .

# BLUE MOON BACKLIST TITLES

## ANONYMOUS

#82 BLUE VELVET           $4.95
Trapped in a Victorian Story of O, Clarissa was trained at her father's knee and her husband's hand to endure everything. But when still others come to take charge, Clarissa turns her power to please into a weapon.

#43 THE CAPTIVE           $5.95
When a wealthy English man-about-town attempts to make advances to the beautiful twenty-year-old debutante Caroline Martin, she haughtily repels him. As revenge, he pays a white-slavery ring £30,000 to have Caroline abducted and spirited away to the remote Atlas Mountains of Morocco. There the mistress of the ring and her sinister assistant Jason begin Caroline's education—an eduction designed to break her will and prepare her for her mentor.

#98 CAPTIVE II            $5.95
Each young woman taken by the agents of Rio 9 to the remote and well-guarded estate of Camba Real pays the price of her arrogance or hostility. The Captive II carries on where The Captive left off.

#123 THE CAPTIVE III      $5.95
The Captive III, the Perfumed Trap, is the story of slavery and passionate training, described first-hand in the spirited correspondence of two wealthy cousins, Alec and Miriam. The power wielded by them over the girls who cross their paths leads them beyond Cheluna to the remote settlement of Cambina Alta and a life of plantation discipline. On the way, Alec's passion for Julie, a golden-haired nymph, is rivalled by Miriam's disciplinary zeal for Jenny, a rebellious young woman under correction at a police barracks.

#57 EVELINE II            $4.50
In this sizzling sequel, she attempts to escape the boredom of marriage by "converting" other young ladies to her wicked ways.

#19 GREEN GIRLS           $4.95
A superb rendition of how well a willing girl can fare at school.

#100 HARDCASTLE           $5.95
You are young, strong and beautiful, Astrid Cane is told, when in the sensuous and knowing hands of Lady Julia Tingle she is brought into the "full" domain of womanhood.

**#94 LUST'S LABOUR WON $4.95**
An elegant mansion is turned into a "school" where Muriel and other young English aristocrats receive unusual instruction in the byways of love. Shy and timorous at first, Muriel and her friends soon learn to take sensual delight in their strict curriculum.

**#88 MAN WITH A MAID II $4.95**
This sequel to one of the most famous erotic novels of Victorian England continues the tale of the sexual adventures of Jack, the gentleman who has been jilted by his beloved Alice and vows to "make her voluptuous person recompense for his disappointment."

**#104 MAN WITH A MAID III $5.95**
This third volume of one of the most famous erotic novels of the Victorian era continues the extraordinary memoirs of the saucy gentleman Jack. He now recounts the great delights of his association with the new and imperious beauty, Helen Hotspur.

**#65 MARISKA I $4.95**
Mariska, beautiful ballerina of the Russian Imperial Theater, becomes legendary for the bizarre uses to which she puts her strong, acrobatic body in gratifying her own and others' desires.

**#73 MARISKA II $4.95**
Mariska's unsparingly graphic journey reveals every detail of her bizarre life of discipline and submission.

**#120 THE MERRY ORDER OF ST. BRIDGET $5.95**
In a series of graphically detailed letters to a friend, Margaret Anson, the young, submissive personal handmaiden to the notorious Marquis St. Valery, describes the bizarre, but personally exciting orgies at the infamous Chateau de Floris.

**#20 MISS HIGH HEELS $4.95**
A young aristocrat is transformed by his step-sister into a beautiful woman and initiated into exquisite pleasures and pains.

**#27 MY SECRET LIFE $9.95**
The famous 640 page sexual memoir of a well-to-do Victorian gentleman, who began at an early age to keep a diary of his erotic behavior. "It shows us that amid and underneath the world of Victorian England as we knew it, a real secret social life was being conducted, the secret life of sexuality." —Steven Marcus, <u>The Other Victorians</u>

**#17 OXFORD GIRL $4.95**
From the moment he arrives at Oxford University, a young American scholar forsakes his previous innocence for a decadent adventure.

#93 PAMELA $4.95
Pamela appeared so alluringly innocent that she had no difficulty at all in acquiring the post of governess and tutor to the daughters of Sir Richard and Lady Bromley at their country estate.

#96 RETURNING HOME $5.95
The dreamily seductive Jenny returns home after a long absence to find her household replete with possibilities of pleasure. Variously coy and domineering, Jennie indulges in her most elaborate fancies.

#116 ROMANCE OF LUST $5.95
The four volumes of The Romance of Lust were first issued between 1873 and 1876. They comprise perhaps the best and the longest erotic novel in existence. The Romance of Lust is the witty first-person account of the sexual education of Charlie Roberts, perhaps the most famous hero of the Victorian underground.

#122 THE VICAR'S GIRL $5.95
In a sedate, rural village in late nineteenth century England, the beautiful Vanessa lived quietly with her brother until the day the lustful local Vicar took her in hand. From then on the proud mistress succumbed to a torrent of pleasure her body had never before known. In time, the modest hamlet became a hotbed of passion, as Vanessa turned her new-found skills to luring other households into their secret coterie.

#31 WEEKEND VISIT $4.95
Here is another volume in perhaps the most famous erotic series of Victorian England, A Man With A Maid. In this sequel, Jack's life takes another fortunate turn when he makes the intimate acquaintance of his deceased friend's daughter, her beautiful mother, and their charming 18-year-old companion.

## CELESTE ARDEN

#67 FANTASY HUNTERS $4.95
A crack team of bawdy women are instructed to delve shamelessly into the dark and secret world of male sexuality.

## ELIZABETH BENNETT

#126 THE AFTERNOONS OF A WOMAN OF LEISURE $5.95
Joanna is a beautiful young woman of leisure. She is married to a bank president much older than herself, and is mildly dissatisfied with her life. The situation is made worse by the fact that her husband no longer seems interested in sleeping with her, and by her own ongoing confusion about

herself. Several chance encounters shock Joanna into action. She becomes involved with a mysterious "O", a woman whose clients and employees experiment with pleasure, pain and what the director refers to as "issues of control". Joanna's experiences with "O" are exciting, but also dangerous. Identities are revealed, alliances shifted and plots undertaken. Joanna begins to gather secrets and to lay the foundation of her terrible revenge: graphic, erotic and ultimately murderous.

## P.N. DEDEAUX

#127 ALGIERS TOMORROW $5.95
The two rich English girls were hot as firecrackers and spoiled as fallen fruit. All of North Africa knew them as The Breast and The Buttocks. Swarthy Lotharios threatened each other with murderous blades for a single chance at their bountiful white flesh, and all the while, the riotous young girls were making the local ladies of the night look like refugees from an Algerian medicare line. Britain had given them culture, and before they left, they almost proved that Britannia Rules...until they ran afoul of white slavery.

#45 CLOTILDA $4.50
Beautiful, blond Clotilda is the acme of English girlhood as we follow her misfortunes through centuries of pain mingled with pleasure, of ecstasy with agony, from the Roman conquest where she was sold as a slave to the 17th century, where she receives a birching from her Victorian curate father.

#44 THE PRUSSIAN GIRLS $4.95
The time is the early 18th century, in a Prussian ladies seminary, where the most vigorous rules pervade, providing corporal correction of its high born pupils and also its mistresses.

#61 TRANSFER POINT-NICE $4.50
Victoria and her school chum Joy, broke on the Riviera, soon find themselves being shuttled from the custody of a depraved dwarf in Nice to the clutches of a lecherous Arab in Algiers.

## EDWARD DELAUNAY

#81 BEATRICE $4.95
A young Victorian woman portrayed not as a cardboard cut-out figure, but seen with all her nuances of shyness and hesitation of desires, Beatrice enters the strange fires of "love and obedience".

#112 BETWEEN THE SHADOWS AND THE LIGHT $5.95
Never was a stranger, more poetic or more powerfully sensuous novel created in the Victorian genre.

#113 DANCING FAWNS $5.95
Fresh from strict but loving care of her headmistress at boarding school, Elizabeth returns home to find an impassioned lover eager to school her further in the delights of the flesh.

#115 THE TANGERINE $5.95
A dreamlike tale of erotic pursuits by lovely young English ladies at the turn of the century.

## WILMA KAUFFEN

#101 VIRTUE'S REWARDS $5.95
A green-eyed voluptuous blonde barely makes ends meet as she turns her boss' dental practice into a huge success, then becomes a porno star. It seems that the kinder and more generous she is to men, the more humiliating punishment she suffers. It's her fate to be "spanked for being good". From the author of *Our Scene*.

## MARIA MADISON

#78 THE ENCOUNTER $4.95
She enacts the total role of being submissive, following his detailed instructions and being punished if she does not. She is beautiful and ultimately masters the "arts" which please him. From the author of *The Reckoning*

#117 WHAT LOVE $5.95
She is thirty, a college instructor quietly married, quietly divorced, alone now, lonely. And then, on the street one night, "I don't notice the man at first, he's like a shadow…a phantom…leaning back in the autumn twilight." And then, when she says "I'm a nice English girl", he says, "I think you've played the good girl for too long, you offend me…you're a naughty girl. Watch out I don't spank you again." She thinks, "I thought only men felt lust. It's animal, it has no conscience. It craves, it hungers. Just like me…This kind of cruel sex is my sin, my guilty secret."

## RICHARD MANTON

#114 DEPARTURE FROM THE GOLDEN CROSS $5.95
This story takes place behind the locked doors of a girls' reformatory to reveal the scandalous escapades of zealous reformers and their wards.

#56 ELAINE COX $4.50
A classic study of obsession in a world of schoolgirl uniforms and correct behavior.

#111 GARDENS OF THE NIGHT $5.95
Casting aside reserve, pride and "good sense", Lesley submits to the perverse demands of her Machiavellian lover Anton.

#09 LA VIE PARISIENNE $4.95
Shuttered rooms of exclusive finishing schools...masters and mistresses matched in their perverse sexuality.

#83 LESLEY $4.95
Lesley makes a strange, dreamlike journey to a beautiful summer villa in Florville. Under the expert guidance of her mentors, Lesley gives herself over to total sensual abandon.

#110 NOREEN $5.95
A novel of obsession in the tradition of the best-selling *Elaine Cox*. Its narrator reveals his sadistic passion for Noreen, "a strapping young trollop" of nineteen.

#64 THE ODALISQUE $4.95
In the high noon of Victorian empire, Lady Jenny Langham accompanies her soldier uncle from the luxuries of London to the Nile city of Khartoum, where Jenny and her maid fall into the hands of the victorious Mahdi and spend long, hot months in erotic captivity.

#89 TRAVELLER'S TALES $4.95
Sensual adventures abound in this unique collection of excerpts from the lustiest Victorian novels illustrating the sexual practices of the harem. They vary from the Dey of Algiers' toying with British "love slaves" to the sensual surprises in the Harem of Sheikh Atra Amani.

#86 TROPIC OF VENUS $4.95
Captian Charles de Vane, educated at Oxford, was in the Army list of 1899 as an officer in South Africa. The military adventures of this gentleman took him to the far reaches of the earth—and to the exotic climes of the most exquisite sexuality.

#118 A VICTORIAN SAMPLER
Edited by Richard Manton $5.95
A masterly collection of Victorian erotic literature, from *My Secret Life* to newly discovered gems such as *Birch in the Boudoir* and *The Days at Florville*. Also included is the best history yet of Victorian erotic literature, the true story of Charles Carrington, the underground publisher of the period, a story as exciting as his books.

#47 VILLA ROSA $4.50
In the final banquet years of a decayed society, three men share a summer's pleasure with their chosen girls.

## AKAHIGE NAMBAN

#15 WOMAN OF THE
MOUNTAIN, WARRIORS
OF THE TOWN                    $4.95
The adventures of Satsuki, a sophisticated courtesan of 17th century Japan, as she and the beautiful blonde prisoner Rosamund persevere through sensual and bloody adventures. A further tale in the legends of the shogun's agents.

#49 SHOGUN'S AGENTS    $4.50
After receiving special rank in the Shogun service, Jira and Geoman's adventures take them to every corner of 17th century Japan and the farthest reaches of erotic delight.

#70 TOKYO STORY          $4.95
Two brothers, Jim Suzuki and Andy Middler, seek the solution to the mystery of their parentage and discover a whole new world of exotic pleasures.

#95 MASTERS OF CLOUDS
AND RAIN                        $4.95
Andy Middler and Jim Suzuki continue their search for the mysterious Cloud and Rain Corp. The two young men travel through rural Japan looking for answers, and find them in strange and sometimes very erotic ways.

#119 YAKUZA PERFUME    $5.95
More erotic adventures of Jim and Andy, two Japanese American brothers who are surprised by a female agent of the Clouds and Rain Corp. who seeks refuge with them. After she leaves they are accused of stealing the secret of the sexually intoxicating pheromone perfume that is the basis of the company's power.

## JAY PARINI

#66 THE LOVE RUN         $4.95
Maisie Danston, a rich, sensuous Dartmouth senior, is at the moist center of this "fast-paced, lucid, sexy novel". —The Times of London

## MARTIN PYX

#58 AUTUMN SCANDALS $4.95
Mona's orgiastic breach of her sorority's dating ban earns her extra retribution.

#124 SPRING FEVERS      $5.95
*"On our weekends, my husband and I play at being 16 year-old cousins."*
Continuing the tale begun in *Summer Frolics* and *Autumn Scandals*, adult role-playing games spice California lives: Professor Porter and swamp spitfire Lucretia Sue ad-lib aphrodesiac punishments required by British-bred enthusiasts of the rod; identities blur as Lady Mildmount from *Thomasina* and

*An English Education's* Jane Eyre retrain a Victorian sex education truant; Sigma Epsilon Xi's toastily paddled sorority hopefuls vie to become pledge princess and weary Hollywood superstar Honey Fitz Sullivan refreshes herself with incestuous siblings, while the curse of a Goddess worshiper falls upon her unchaste son and his deceived concubine.

#52  SUMMER FROLICS    $4.50
By the steaming Persian Gulf, the eunuch who read Hemingway teaches Lucretia Sue the ecstasy and anguish of unendurable pleasure indefinitely prolonged. Juliana, wife to the English consul, discovers the pangs of the White Woman's Burden in an Arab sheikdom.

#30  THE TUTOR'S BRIDE  $4.95
A sun-scalded Caribbean isle welcomes New England bride Dolly Hunter. Both sexes delight as she explores local fusions of casual French libertinage and correct English discipline.

## DAVID REDSHAW

#75  BITCH WITCH    $4.95
Set in 18th century London, this is one of the most unusual tales of domination. Elizabeth Anderson, a dominatrix of old England uses every trick in the book. From the author of *In The Mist*

## LAURENCE ST. CLAIR

#53 ISABELLE & VERONIQUE  $4.50
Manhattan, Paris, London and Rome are the settings for this modern erotic triangle. A sophisticated story of intrigue and passion.

## BRIONY SHILTON

#125 SUNDANCER    $5.95
In this contemporary story, Sundancer, so named by her captor, is deserted by her boyfriend in a strange hotel in a strange city in the care of a little grey man, who transports her to his house as his prisoner. She is held there under a both physically and emotionally hypnotic eroticism. Punishment and care alternate until an ultimate violent awakening.

## JACK SPENDER

#45  PROFESSOR SPENDER AND
THE SADISTIC IMPULSE    $4.50
Hired to teach amoral sorority honeys in the French Riviera sun, Professor Spender regiments their heedless sexual frolics under the brooding, lustful shadow of the Marquis de Sade.

#26 THE RITES OF SODOM  $4.95
Irrepressible Professor Jack Spender is off again, this time to unearth the ancient city of Sodom.

## DANIEL VIAN

#54 THE HOUR OF THE WOLF: PARIS 1941  $4.50
In the occupied city the Nazis are the masters and Simone and Bernard are determined to make the most of the opportunity in their new world order.

#48 WINKLER: BERLIN 1923  $4.50
In Weimer Berlin the cabarets were full but there were things happening in Germany not so easy to sing about.

## DON WINSLOW

#121 THE HIDDEN GALLERY  $5.95
A most unusual portfolio of exceptional women, a rare collection of portraits whose captivating subjects are carefully rendered in loving detail and exquisitely presented in vibrant sexual tableaux. By the author of *Ironwood*.

#46 IRONWOOD REVISITED  $4.50
This exciting sequel to Ironwood reveals how that unique institution acquired its premier reputation for iron discipline.

#22 IRONWOOD  $4.95
The harsh reality of James' world as a disinherited heir vanishes when he discovers he's in line for a choice position at an exclusive and very strict school for girls. Ironwood becomes for him a fantastic dream world where discipline knows few boundaries, and where his role as master affords him free reign.

#63 IMAGES OF IRONWOOD  $4.95
The third volume of the infamous Ironwood trilogy offers scenes of unrelenting sexuality, of erotic longings, and occasionally, of those bizarre proclivities which touch the outer fringe of human sexuality.

# Sundancer
## Briony Shilton

"Right. In future you will do PRECISELY what I tell you, and no more. Understand this—you have no name until I give you one. You have no possessions unless I give them to you. Your body is not yours, but mine. If I wish to thrash you daily, I will. You will not fight but accept without screaming for mercy. You will scream. I shall not feel I have done the job properly unless you do, but you won't plead or say no. Do you understand? I cannot control your thoughts, no doubt they are full of hatred for me at the moment! You hate me all right, but in time, in time you will hate your boyfriend more, for he knew what he was handing to me when he signed the contract. Long have I wanted to initiate someone into the joys of submission!"

BLUE MOON • 125 • (CANADA $6.95) • U.S. $5.95

# WHAT LOVE

## Maria Madison

She is thirty, a college instructor quietly married, quietly divorced, alone now, lonely. And then, on the street one night, "I don't notice the man at first, when I see him, he's like a shadow . . . a phantom . . . leaning back into the autumn twilight." And when they speak, he says later, "You're a teacher . . . you don't look the part . . . You're too delicate."

And then, when she says "I'm a nice English girl", he says, "I think you've played the good girl for too long, you offend me . . . you're a naughty girl. Watch out I don't spank you again."

She thinks, "I thought only men felt lust. It's animal, it has no conscience. It craves, it hungers. Just like me . . . This kind of cruel sex is my sin, my guilty secret." He says to a friend, "She's an object I enjoy. I get a tremendous kick from beating her. It turns me on." And she says, "I am a clean wiped slate, needing education. Special education". The author has published with Blue Moon two other books, *The Reckoning* and *The Encounter*.

BLUE MOON • 125 • (CANADA $6.95) • U.S. $5.95

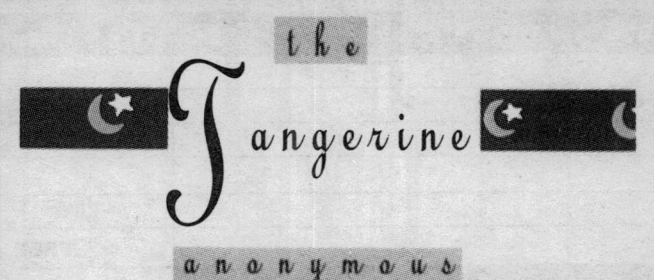

# the Tangerine

## anonymous

A dreamlike tale of erotic pursuits by lovely young English ladies at the turn of the century. Whether aboard the yacht, The Tangerine or in their own abodes, all traits lead them to pleasure and amusement.

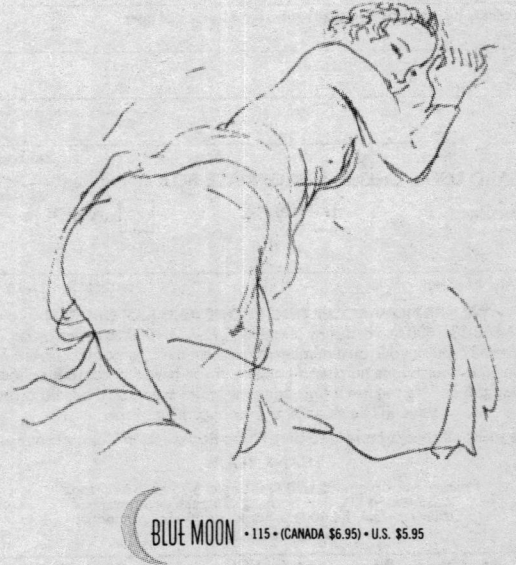

BLUE MOON • 115 • (CANADA $6.95) • U.S. $5.95

# ORDER FIVE BOOKS RECEIVE ONE BOOK FREE!

| Bk# | Title | Qty. | Price |
|---|---|---|---|
| | | | |
| | | | |
| | | | |
| | | | |
| | | | **FREE** |
| | | Subtotal | |
| | | Postage and Handling | |
| | Tax (N.Y. and PA. Residents only add 8.25%) | | |
| | | Total $ | |

Signature (I certify by my signature that I am over 21 years of age)

Name

Address

City                                State                        Zip code

CREDIT CARD USERS CHECK APPROPRIATE BOX

☐ MasterCard            ☐ VISA            ☐ AMEX

Credit Card Number                        / Expiration Date

### WE ARE NOW ACCEPTING PHONE AND FAX ORDERS!

Call us at 1-800-535-0007 to order by phone or 212-673-1039 to order by fax 7 days a week. We will require your card number, expiration date, name and current mailing address. Include your phone number if possible. If you have any questions about your order please call us. We request a <u>four book minimum</u> credit card order. Forthcoming titles will be shipped as they become available.

Please make all checks payable to Blue Moon Books Inc. in U.S. currency only

THANK YOU!

Postage Information: $1.50 first book  $.75 each additional
Canada: $2.00 first book  $1.25 each additional
Other foreign: $4.00 first book  $2.00 each additional
<u>NO C.O.D. ORDERS</u>

---

**Blue Moon Books** Published by: Blue Moon Books, Inc.
P.O. Box 1040, Cooper Station, New York, NY 10276
Phone: 212/505-6880 or 1-800/535-0007 Fax: 212/673-1039